King's Crown

Book 20

Twin Soul series

King's Crown

Winner Twins

And

Todd McCaffrey

Summary: The saga of the King's War continues.

Cover art by Jeff Winner

Books by The Winner Twins and Todd McCaffrey

Nonfiction:

The Write Path: World Building

Books by McCaffrey-Winner

Twin Soul Series:

TS1 - Winter Wyvern

TS2 - Cloud Conqueror

TS3 - Frozen Sky

TS4 - Wyvern's Fate

TS5 - Wyvern's Wrath

TS6 - Ophidian's Oath

TS7 - Snow Serpent

TS8 - Iron Air

TS9 - Ophidian's Honor

TS10 - Healing Fire

TS11 - Ophidian's Tears

TS12 - Cloud War

TS13 - Steel Waters

TS14 - Cursed Mage

TS15 - Wyvern's Creed

TS16 - King's Challenge

TS17 - King's Conquest

TS18 - King's Treasure

TS19 - Wyvern Rider

Books by Todd McCaffrey

Science fiction

Ellay

The Jupiter Game

Collections

The One Tree of Luna (And Other Stories)

Dragonriders of Pern® Series

Dragon's Kin

Dragon's Fire

Dragon Harper

Dragonsblood

Dragonheart

Dragongirl

Dragon's Time

Sky Dragons

Non-fiction

Dragonholder: The Life And Times of Anne McCaffrey

Dragonwriter: A tribute to Anne McCaffrey and Pern

Books by The Winner Twins

Nonfiction:

The Write Path: Navigating Storytelling

Science Fiction:

The Strand Prophecy

Extinction's Embrace

PCT: Perfect Compatibility Test

Dedication

For Miguel Sandoval.

An incredible son, husband, and father.

A true fighter.

Map

Contents

Prolog

eter Hewlitt, Kingsland's spymaster, was glad when he heard footsteps approaching the scratch-built shack where he'd been on guard. In the hour since the others had left, the girl seemed to have gotten worse, fainter, weaker. He'd discovered, to his dismay, that she was particularly susceptible to the sound of his voice. Apologetically, Matt Evans had explained that Peter's voice was similar to that of the Steam Master's, blocking and moving into Hewlitt's space to force the spymaster to move away.

"Who's that?" Travers demanded when he heard the approaching sounds.

"They're back," Hewlitt said, moving toward the door.

Travers jumped in front of him, blocking his way. "Don't do that! It can't be them, it's too soon!"

Hewlitt was the king's spymaster. With two quick jabs, he had the railman on the ground, holding his sides and writhing in agony.

Nelly was unsympathetic, looking up from her kneeling position beside the stricken girl, she tsked, saying to the groaning Travers, "Really, you should know better!"

The door burst open, and a young girl strode in, moving with determination.

"Margiss, what are you doing here?" Freddie Fennimore said.

"It's Bethany Margiss now," Bethany replied with Margiss' voice. She moved past him and knelt beside Nelly, nodding to the older woman before turning her attention to Barbara. She stroked the girl's hair softly and said, "We're here, we came as soon as we could."

Nelly found herself suddenly crying and didn't understand why until she saw tears rolling down the young girl's face and realized that her knee was touching Margiss'. The moment she pulled away from her, the intense pain and emotion left her. "How do you do that?"

"Do what?" Bethany Margiss replied, still intent on Barbara. "Barbara, dear, we're here. We're here to help."

Others entered the room and Nelly was relieved to have Jarin Reedis touch her shoulder lightly in an unspoken

King's Crown

inquiry. Nelly knelt back and stood, turning to embrace the twin-souled man who hugged tightly in return.

"She's broken," Travers said with a soft giggle, rising from the floor while keeping his distance from Hewlitt.

"So are you," Annabelle said with Ellen's voice. She turned back to Bethany Margiss and gestured toward Barbara. "I need to tend to her wounds."

Margiss nodded and moved over. Margaret hissed as she took in the other girl's state. She took an involuntary step back and turned away. Ellen Annabelle shot a look in her direction but, with a firm nod, put the older girl's discomfort out of her mind and returned her gaze to the injured Barbara.

Annabelle knelt down and turned back to the rest of the room. "She's going to want her privacy."

The men glanced at each other uncomfortably.

"I can make a fire," Ophidian promised. The railmen, who until that moment had not noticed the dragon god, found themselves moving hastily to the door without quite knowing why. Soon, only Ellen, Margiss, and Nelly remained behind.

Prolog 15

"Can you stand guard?" Ellen said to Skara, who had just that moment walked through the door.

"Who are you talking to?" Nelly said, giving the young twin soul a surprised look.

"She can't see me," Skara said to Ellen. She made a face. "I think only those who have seen death can see me."

"Well, she saw you die," Bethany Margiss told her. She touched Nelly's hand. "Nelly Kendral, meet Skara Ningan."

Nelly's eyes widened as she could suddenly see the other woman. "You were the one they killed!"

"Yes," Skara admitted dourly. "Thomas is outside with the men."

"But the door didn't open!" Nelly said, glancing from Skara to the door behind her.

Skara grinned impishly. "Yes," she said, "pretty amazing, isn't it?"

Nelly nodded mutely.

"One of the perks of being dead," Skara said.

"Shh!" Annabelle hushed. "We need to roll her over, lift her shirt —"

"Or cut it — " Margiss said.

King's Crown

"Lift it unless you've got a replacement," Annabelle continued. She glanced to Bethany Margiss. "I may need your help with the healing."

"Healing?" Nelly said.

"It's a secret far too many people are learning," Skara said with a sour glance toward Ellen Annabelle. "Little Ellen brought Annabelle back to life as a wyvern and twinned with her."

Nelly looked at the little girl with respect. "You did?"

Ellen nodded, her cheeks flushed.

"She can heal others," Bethany Margiss agreed.

"You took those poisoned teeth," Nelly pointed out.

Margiss nodded and jerked a hand toward Ellen. "She does physical healing better than me."

"And you?"

"She heals the mind," a new voice spoke up. The five women turned to the sound and saw a woman dressed in pale colors standing before them. Skara moved to protect the others, but Bethany Margiss stopped her with a curt gesture.

"Goddess," Bethany Margiss said, bowing her head quickly and glancing for the others to do the same.

Prolog

"Goddess?" Skara said questioningly, not moving from her defensive position.

"Kahlas," the goddess replied. She smiled at Margiss. "Well sensed, newborn."

"Please," Ellen Annabelle begged, "let me heal this one."

"That's why I'm here," Kahlas agreed, though she kept her eyes on Margiss. She waved for Ellen to proceed. Ellen made an imploring gesture to Nelly who quickly caught on that the seven-year-old body was not suited to turning the older teenaged body over. Gently, she helped Ellen and Margiss roll the injured girl over.

"Allow me," Kahlas said, moving forward. With a wave of her hand, the back part of Barbara's shirt disappeared, revealing ugly welts. Margaret turned around and made a horrified sound.

"You were worse," Bethany Margiss told her. Margaret's eyes went dark. "We can help her, don't worry."

Margaret nodded and moved to stand behind Ellen Annabelle. Ellen reached back a hand. Margaret took it and the younger girl squeezed it once in comfort and let it go.

King's Crown

"You can add your magic to hers," Kahlas said to Margaret in a kindly tone. "Just touch her and think to add your strength."

"My magic is mostly air," Margaret said.

Kahlas nodded. "I know."

Margaret gulped as she recalled that she was talking to a god. She touched Ellen's shoulder. The little girl patted her hand once in assurance, then moved her hands to hover over the injuries on Barbara's back. Bethany Margiss moved closer to Ellen Annabelle and laid a hand on the smaller girl's arm, closing her eyes.

Ellen turned to Kahlas, "Is there anything else I should do?"

Kahlas smiled at her. "I don't know," Kahlas told her. She glanced toward Margaret. "Your friend might know better."

"I was in too much pain to even think," Margaret admitted ruefully. She gently squeezed Ellen's shoulder. "Whatever you did last time worked."

Ellen nodded in understanding, eyes still closer.

Fortunately, Barbara's physical injuries were less than Margaret's had been. In a few scant minutes, the wounds

Prolog

closed, the skin healed, and bruises disappeared. Ellen let out a deep breath and leaned back against Margaret, exhausted.

"It is the mind that will be more difficult," Kahlas said, magically returning the back half of Barbara's shirt to her body.

"What do I need to do?" Bethany Margiss asked, moving closer to the still form on the cot.

"You need to come with me," Kahlas said. "Ophidian?"

"I hear you," the dragon god said, standing inside the room as though he'd never left. "What do you propose?"

"I am one of the guardians of the mind," Kahlas said. She nodded toward Bethany Margiss. "If she wishes it, I could teach her much."

"In exchange for what, exactly?" Nelly said, moving to stand by Bethany Margiss.

"Oh! Aren't you a proper guardian!" Kahlas said, her lips turning up in delight. She turned to Ophidian. "Do you claim her?"

"My heart belongs with Reedis," Nelly snapped back. In a softer voice, she added, "And Jarin, his twin soul."

King's Crown

"So you are half-dragon, but not wholly so," Kahlas said to herself. She met Nelly's eyes. The woman stared back unflinchingly.

"Miss Kendral, you should know that Kahlas is the goddess of the moon and the inner eye," Ophidian said in a tone that was mild but conveyed a warning.

"I am not afraid of gods," Nelly replied staunchly.

"Yes," Ophidian agreed with a sigh, "I'd noticed."

Kahlas laughed. She waved a hand toward Nelly. "I mean no harm to you and yours, mage."

"I'm not — I mean, I don't — " Nelly stammered. She broke half and gave the goddess a quick curtsy. "Thank you."

"Back to this deal," Skara Ningan said, moving to stand by Nelly protectively. The school principal gave her a grateful look.

"The dead walk?" Kahlas said, turning to Ophidian.

"I made a deal," Ophidian said, nodding toward Ellen and Margiss. "They need protecting."

"That is why I am here," Kahlas said. She nodded toward Bethany Margiss. "She has potential, as you know, but she is untrained."

"You offer to train her?" Skara demanded. "How?"

"Why is it a concern of yours, dead human?"

"She was once my twin soul," Bethany spoke up quickly, her eyes flashing. "I love her as a sister, if not more."

Skara's face burst into a huge grin. She nodded, eyes misting in fervent agreement with the young twin soul.

"Spymaster Hewlitt," Kahlas' voice rose to carry through the door and into the winds outside the hut.

"Am I wanted?" Hewlitt replied, knocking on the door. "Miss Kendral?"

"Come," Nelly replied.

Hewlitt opened the door and strode through, followed on his heels by Margen and, oddly, Travers.

"Yes, yes, I see you," Kahlas said as soon as Travers caught sight of her. She turned to Ophidian and gave him the sort of exasperated expression that only one god can give to another. Ophidian buried his grin in a thin-lipped grimace.

"Do you recall a young lad lately in the service of the queen?" Kahlas demanded of the spymaster, her eyes still on Bethany Margiss.

King's Crown

"The one she alternately called 'Britches' and 'No Britches'?"

"What?" Nelly demanded. She turned to Hewlitt. "How old was this lad?"

"He had a sister," Kahlas continued, ignoring Nelly's outburst. She turned to catch Hewlitt's eyes. "They had fled from Jasram to prevent her from marrying against her will."

"I was not aware of that," Hewlitt said, pursing his lips in thought. He glanced to the goddess. "Casman?"

Kahlas nodded.

"Casman!" Ophidian said. He turned to Kahlas. "Now things become clearer."

"It helps that I can see the whole world, not just the parts that interest me at one particular moment," Kahlas said high-mindedly.

"Which reminds me," Ophidian began, "I have —"

"Yes, I know," Kahlas said. "And it would be best not to forestall her journey much longer."

"Ibb said —"

Prolog  23

"You speak with the metal ones?" Kahlas interjected. When Ophidian nodded, she continued in a lower tone, "I cannot scry what they think."

"Understandably," Ophidian agreed. "But Ibb and Tracker are helping me on a project which might help your pet on her way."

"She's no pet!" Kahlas replied hotly. When she noticed the satisfaction in Ophidian's eyes, she shook her head. In a soft tone, she continued, "If you'd just asked me, I would have told you the same."

"But now I know," Ophidian replied.

"Are you two going to keep entertaining yourselves for the rest of the day?" Jarin Reedis demanded as he walked in. "Or is something of import going to be said, or some action taken?"

"Oh, *he's* your son!" Kahlas said to Ophidian with glee.

"She's getting around to making us an offer," Bethany Margiss said, glancing toward Margen. "I think she wants us to join her on the moon."

"Yes, exactly," Kahlas agreed. She turned to Ophidian, noting the other's growing ire. "At least, at first. After…"

"Can you help her?" Margaret Waters spoke up, moving to stand beside Bethany Margiss but pointing toward Barbara Garrett. The young teen was sleeping peacefully, her muscles unclenched.

"And him?" Nelly said, nodding toward Travers.

"And you want help for your Casman children," Hewlitt guessed.

"Oh, look, it's Kahlas!" Wymarc said acidly as Krea Wymarc stepped through the door. She turned back to the remaining railmen and said, "You'd best stay outside, unless you want to go mad."

"Oh, hello, Wymarc," Kahlas said. "Didn't recognize you in the new body?" She scanned Krea's albino form quickly and scowled. "Bit of a step down for you, isn't it?"

"You dare!" Wymarc hissed, her words echoed by Jarin Reedis.

"Kahlas, really," Ophidian said in a mild voice. "Were you not once all white yourself?"

"And I remember the scorn applied to me by a young daughter of yours," Kahlas said, nodding coldly toward Wymarc.

"I apologize," Krea said. "Wymarc was younger then, and hadn't the chance —"

"I apologize," Wymarc said, taking control of Krea's voice. "I was wrong." She lifted her eyes up to meet Kahlas'. "Will you forgive me?"

Kahlas' eyes widened in shock. A moment later she said, "Of course I'll forgive you." She turned back to Ophidian. "They do grow up, don't they?"

Ophidian acknowledged this with a dip of his chin. "As to your offer…?"

Kahlas turned back to Bethany Margiss and knelt down. "Young wyvern, yours is a gift given only rarely and it could help so many. Would you please let me teach you all that I can?"

"The last one was… Aldara," Ophidian recalled.

"Aldara the Addled?" Wymarc snapped, her eyes going wide. She looked beseechingly to Ophidian. "Father, you can't —"

"Aldara lived a long time, a very long time ago," Kahlas said, "when the gods themselves were very different." Kahlas looked over to Bethany Margiss. "She had my training, but

she was overwhelmed in the end." Kahlas made a gesture toward Ophidian. "During the God's War."

"Could this happen to Bethany Margiss, too?" Skara asked in a small voice.

"It could," Kahlas agreed. "Nothing is guaranteed." She nodded to Bethany Margiss, adding, "And there are gods arrayed against you. There are gods who like to break men's minds, to hurt, to maim —"

"Please, goddess!" Travers begged. "Please."

"And sometimes," Kahlas said with a wave toward Travers who broke off and curled up in a ball, whimpering, "sometimes they bring it on themselves."

"What else?" Nelly demanded. "You threaten this child's sanity, tell her that gods might want to torture her, why are you here?"

"It's the children," Hewlitt said, nodding to Kahlas. Kahlas turned her head toward him and tilted an eyebrow upwards. "The children of the moon."

"Too many are dead," Kahlas said in agreement, her voice sad. She glanced over to Ophidian. "Your children live, grow, and prosper…"

Prolog

"That is because of her," Ophidian said, nodding to Ellen Annabelle. She turned bright red. Ophidian added softly, "And because *humans* took pity on her and helped her live."

"That is what I'm asking for," Kahlas said. "Pity."

"You know Hana, don't you?" Krea spoke up. "You are the goddess of the —"

Kahlas stopped her with an upraised hand. "Few people know, it is a secret, perhaps forever."

"Not if we can help it," Krea spoke up fiercely. "I gave a vow —"

"And *that*, too, should be kept a secret," Kahlas warned. She turned her eyes back to Bethany Margiss. "What I am offering is a chance to learn to help injuries of the brain and the mind, a chance to heal the inner eye, a rare gift only suited to those with rare talents."

"And if she refuses?" Skara demanded.

"And what of Chandra?" Bethany Margiss demanded.

"Who?"

"Her rider," Wymarc explained. She jerked her head toward the door. "She is, apparently, sensible to —"

 King's Crown

The door opened, and Chandra stomped in, glaring at Ophidian, then Kahlas.

"Chandra Earthshaker, may I make you known to Kahlas, goddess of the moon," Ophidian said with a chortle.

"Earthshaker?"

"She broke the gates of the zwerg kingdom in the north, looking for someone to help me," Margaret Waters explained, beaming with pride toward her adopted sister. She waved a hand toward Bethany Margiss. "You don't get one without the other."

Kahlas turned wide eyes toward Ophidian. "You would have me take an *earth* mage to the moon?"

Ophidian shrugged. "Not my choice."

Skara shot Chandra an inquiring look. The dark girl explained, "I was keeping the others from entering." She nodded toward Kahlas. "Besides, there was far too much drama already."

"It's the children who worry you," Hewlitt spoke up. Chandra shot him a look, which he ignored. "What is going on in Jasram?"

Prolog 29

"An excellent question," Kahlas allowed. "Are you not the king's spymaster?"

"I have enough to do, keeping up with what is going on in the kingdom," Hewlitt admitted, spreading his hands in a gesture of helplessness.

"Kingdoms, now," Kahlas reminded him. Hewlitt accepted the correction with a grimace and asked, "But the children?"

"They, too, are broken and need help only *we* —" she gestured between herself and Bethany Margiss "— can give."

"She'd be safer," Ophidian said diplomatically.

"On the moon?" Chandra asked. She turned to Kahlas. "Would my magic not work there?"

"'Earth' includes anything you can touch," Kahlas told her. "You magic would work perfectly well up there — perhaps too well."

"How do we get there?" Bethany Margiss asked. She glanced toward Margen. "And could others visit?"

"I'm afraid that we'll be rather busy down here," Margen told his granddaughter apologetically. "But it is a chance of a lifetime, to journey to the goddess' home in the sky."

  King's Crown

"Mr. Travers," Bethany Margiss said, moving toward the man. Travers craned his head back over his shoulder and looked up at her. "Let me see if I can help you."

Travers whimpered and turned his head back to the ground, but he did not resist when Bethany Margiss touched him lightly on the neck. She gave a hiss of pain before clenching her jaw, but she did not flinch away from the man. She made a quick gesture behind her back with her hand and said softly, "Chandra, can you make the ground shake, softly?"

Chandra's eyes widened. She moved toward Bethany Margiss, knelt and closed her eyes. Softly, gently, the shack began to shake.

Travers let out a whimper, then a sigh. Bethany Margiss muttered soft, soothing nonsense words to the man and then sat back, taking her hand from his neck and turning to Chandra. "You can stop now."

"You are good," Kahlas said. "I can feel his ease from here."

"He'll never be completely better," Margiss said, her eyes moist, "but I did what I could."

Prolog

"His injuries are hard to heal," Kahlas said in agreement. One corner of her lips twitched upwards. "He calls to me often and I do what I can, give him dreams and comfort."

Bethany Margiss nodded and stood, grabbing Chandra's hand in her own. "I would like to learn more."

Kahlas raised an eyebrow at Ophidian.

"I do not release any oaths or vows," Ophidian warned his sister god. "And you *will* keep in touch."

"As you say," Kahlas agreed. She raised her hands, palms up, to the two girls.

"Grandfather?" Margiss called out.

"Go!" Margen told her, smiling fondly. "You know how to contact me."

Margiss' eyes widened, and she smiled fiercely. She reached forward and placed her hand, palm down, in Kahlas'. Chandra's hand joined the goddess' other hand.

And the three vanished.

King's Crown

Chapter One

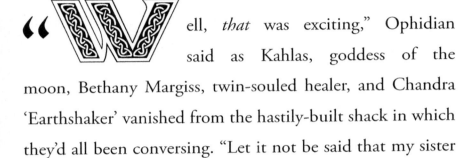

"**W**ell, *that* was exciting," Ophidian said as Kahlas, goddess of the moon, Bethany Margiss, twin-souled healer, and Chandra 'Earthshaker' vanished from the hastily-built shack in which they'd all been conversing. "Let it not be said that my sister doesn't know how to make an exit."

His expression changed when he glanced toward the cot where Barbara Garrett lay, sleeping peacefully, and frowned. "Hmm, apparently she forgot —"

He broke off as the girl's form grew transparent and then invisible, and the blanket thrown over her collapsed.

"I was wondering about that, too," Nelly said, before suddenly pressing her hands to her face and exclaiming, "Oh, heavens! Look at the time! We must get back to mother!"

"Drake!" Wymarc cried as she turned and banged the hut's door open. "Get ready, we're leaving!"

"But what about the railway?" Norman Gossett pleaded.

"Yes," Hewlitt added, glancing toward Ophidian, "what about the railway?"

"You know," Ophidian said in a dangerously soft voice, "I don't owe you anything."

"No," Hewlitt agreed hastily. "In fact, you have been too kind. But I cannot help but think that you, the god of change, are not uninterested in seeing what happens when the rail lines connect all the cities and towns of Kingsland."

Ophidian gave him a look.

"I suspect he's right, you know," Margen chimed in. "Think of all it could do."

"And the airships!" Reedis added. "What wonders will they bring!"

"With airships, why would you need rails?" Ophidian asked slyly.

"Rails for heavy goods moving slowly, airships for lighter goods moving fast," Hewlitt replied immediately. Ophidian looked surprised. The spymaster shrugged. "I have been thinking about this a lot, recently."

"Apparently," Ophidian agreed drolly.

"How long would it take to finish the line to Sorellay?" Hewlitt asked Gossett, the rail boss.

Gossett shrugged. "Without magic —"

"With magic," Margen interrupted. He glanced toward Margaret. "I'd heard it said that you are something to behold, young lady."

Margaret blushed.

"And it wouldn't hurt to learn from the best," Drake piped up faithfully. He glanced at Matt Evans, the other air mage.

"It would be a learning experience," Margen agreed. He glanced toward Nelly. "But, my dear —"

"If you wish to stay here, mage, I think I could take a hand at teaching," Wymarc allowed.

"She's very good," Ellen Annabelle quickly added. "And I'll be safer here than I would at the school."

"Weellll," Nelly said slowly. She glanced at Jarin Reedis. "Do you suppose you could teach a class?"

"Your school *is* named after him," Jarin said.

"I'd be delighted," Reedis allowed. "I can teach balloon magic."

Chapter One

"He can," Ellen Annabelle agreed, "he taught us."

"He did?" Ophidian repeated. He glanced toward Reedis. "And why is this the first I've heard of it?"

"Well, I wouldn't say that you're too busy talking to hear anything," Wymarc replied. "I'll say instead that perhaps you were too *involved* in other matters."

Ophidian fumed at her. Wymarc, with a thousand years' experience, met his gaze staunchly.

"So it's settled," Nelly declared, grabbing Reedis' arm and pulling him out the door. "We'll go back to school — mother will be *much* relieved — and leave you to it."

"And you?" Ophidian demanded of Hewlitt.

"Can you carry… four?" Hewlitt asked Ellen Annabelle. The young girl nodded firmly. Hewlitt smiled at her. He turned to Ophidian. "If it pleases you, I shall remain here. I have never seen railway track laid and I would relish the experience."

"Be careful, spy, you've all the makings of a decent mage," Ophidian warned. Before Hewlitt could react, the dragon god disappeared.

  King's Crown

"Sire, I have good news," first minister Mannevy said as he entered the royal chambers that afternoon.

"Finally," Queen Rassa muttered.

"The airship has returned?" King Markel guessed, frowning as he tried to remember their previous conversation. "You found more money?"

"Not... exactly," the first minister temporized. "However, I *have* discovered a way in which we can get you coronated immediately."

"And how is that?" King Markel said. "You told me that we didn't have enough money."

"And we do not," Mannevy agreed. "But, as we know we will shortly have enough money to pay for the coronation, I discovered a number of your new subjects who were willing to loan us the funds on the promise of the gold when it arrives."

"Why not just take it from them?" Markel wondered.

Mannevy gave him a pained look. "The thought had crossed my mind, sire," the first minister admitted, "but I

thought perhaps you might want to be able to have future dealings with these good people."

"We can always declare them traitors later," Queen Rassa allowed, "and take *all* their money."

"Indeed," Mannevy allowed, looking even more pained, "that is possible. However, I advise against it as it would bring suspicion on the integrity of the crown."

"As long as I *get* my crown, I don't care," King Markel said. He smiled at his minister and rubbed his hands. "When can we do it?"

"Arrangements still take time, sire," Mannevy warned. "But, with this news — perhaps tomorrow evening?"

"Excellent!"

"You can teach?" Mrs. Kendral said when Reedis and the rest returned. When mage Reedis nodded affirmatively, Mrs. Kendral waved him down a corridor. "Room Three."

Reedis shot a look at Nelly who pursed her lips to speak but she was cut off by her mother, who told her, "You have several parents waiting in your lobby."

 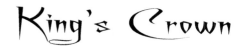 King's Crown

"My lobby?" Nelly squeaked. She didn't know she had a lobby.

"Angry?" Wymarc asked.

"Hopeful," Mrs. Kendral replied enigmatically. She frowned at Wymarc in Krea's body. "Were you hoping to teach as well?"

"Krea is young, but Wymarc is thousands of years old," Reedis told his future mother-in-law.

"Ah!" Mrs. Kendral responded. She gestured down the hall. "If you can take on the class in room Five, then."

"Of course," Krea Wymarc replied, hastening away.

"Well, that's settled," Mrs. Kendral said primly. She turned to her daughter. "If you can manage here, dear, I shall take myself off to the Steam Master's office."

"Office?"

"Yes," Mrs. Kendral said. "I am *very* interested in his bookkeeping."

"The Steam Master said you were the best," Freddie said as he walked with Margaret Waters to the ruins of their

Chapter One ③⑨

construction site. "He used to give Barbara *such* a hard time. He'd always say, 'Margaret can do it better! Why can't you be like her, rich girl?'"

Ellen, who was walking beside them, touched Margaret on the arm. The taller girl looked down at her and Ellen smiled.

"I don't think I am that great," Margaret said, reaching down to take Ellen's hand. "I just do my best, is all."

"That's what Barbara did," Matt Evans said softly. He was trailing just behind them. Further back were the rail crew, mage Margen, and the spymaster, Peter Hewlitt.

Margaret stopped and dropped Ellen's hand, smiling apologetically. To Freddie, she said, "I always call on the gods before I start."

She glanced at the jumble of railroad ties, at the scattered lengths of steel rails. She turned back to the rail boss, Mr. Gossett. "How is the track to be laid?"

"Straight for the next league," Mr. Gossett replied. "But you don't have to worry about all that —"

 King's Crown

"A league I can manage," Margaret told him. She eyed the sky. "It will be getting dark soon enough. We'll lay the league and see what comes next."

Gossett gave her a wide-eyed look. "Whatever you say, miss," he said, his tone doubtful.

Margaret turned to Ellen and smiled. She took three steps forward and knelt on one knee. She closed her eyes and brought her arms up imploringly. "I call upon the gods of the air. Hissia, Hanor, hear my plea!"

She stood, her arms still outstretched. "Please help me show my friends your power. Please let me bear your servant."

"Really?" a voice spoke up from behind her. "But did you not swear service to that child there?"

Margaret spun around and bowed to the goddess of air, Hissia. "She saved my life."

"And now you are hers," Hissia sniffed.

"She was in pain, I helped," Ellen said, moving forward and bowing her head to the goddess.

"You have chosen her as your rider," another voice, male, spoke up from behind Ellen.

Chapter One

"If something happens to me, I want Annabelle to have the best," Ellen said, turning to face Hanor, the god of air. She waved a hand toward Margaret. "And I think she *is* the best."

"She's got you there, dear," Hissia said, amused. She gave Ellen a probing look. "You smell of Rabel."

"He helped me, I am learning from him," Ellen agreed politely. She raised her eyes toward Margaret. "As I hope to learn from Margaret."

"You are a healer, is that not enough?" Hanor asked.

"We are becoming a sorcerer," Annabelle said with Ellen's voice. "There are those who would cause hurt and find our power a source of dread."

"There are more who would see you dead than you guess," Hanor said.

"We stand as their guardian," Thomas Walpish said, moving forward to stand stalwart in front of Ellen. Skara Ningan took her place beside him.

"Oh!" Hissia's eyes widened. She looked to Hanor. "It seems Death has taken an interest in this affair."

King's Crown

"Please, great gods," Margaret said, clasping her hands together and bowing, "we wish only to help." She waved at the timbers and the rails. "With these tracks we can join this country together, make it easier for people to meet, to learn, to honor you."

"Honor us?" Hanor repeated, his tone doubtful.

"When the trains move, the air rushes past," Peter Hewlitt said as he strode forward to join the group. "Then everyone can feel your power."

"Hmm," Hanor allowed, glancing toward Hissia to gauge her reaction.

"I would only honor you," Margaret said beseechingly.

"And your vow to this girl?"

"These women," Annabelle corrected gently with Ellen's voice. "We asked Margaret to be the rider, the one who would bond with the wyvern should anything happen —"

"Enough," Hanor said, waving the girl to silence. "Do you not think, little Ellen, that we didn't hear you call the new-made wyvern to you? That we did not know that you pulled her from the skies with nothing more than your will?"

"And love," Ellen said. "She gave her life to save me."

Chapter One 43

"And love," Hissia said in agreement.

Hanor, god of air, leaned forward and spoke down into Ellen's ear, "We saw it all, little one, never fear."

"Could we learn your magic, too?" Ellen asked in reply. She pointed to herself and moved her hand in such a way that it included both her and Annabelle.

Hissia knelt down so that her words focused on Ellen's other ear. "Of course."

"Ophidian is our brother in many ways," Hanor allowed. The two gods straightened back up. "Watch and learn, little one."

"Margaret," Hissia said to the older girl, a smile playing on her lips.

"Oh, thank you!" Margaret replied, jumping up with joy. "I'll do my best, I promise!"

"It's all we ask, wyvern rider," Hanor replied. He smiled at her and then slowly blew away. Hissia followed a moment later.

Margaret leaned down to whisper in Ellen's ear, "They're still here."

"I guessed," Annabelle replied.

Margaret straightened up and turned to the others. "All honor to Hissia and Hanor. They shall allow my magic today."

The others knelt and bowed their heads, shouting, "All honor!"

Margaret turned back away from them and surveyed the job at hand. She crouched once more, raised her arms above her head and then dropped them straight in front of her. Winds twirled in circles from the ends of her hands. The winds tore through the snow in front of her, raising it in giant whorls that filled the sky. The snow swirled higher and higher and fell away, revealing the bare frozen ground in a long straight line. A line that ran a full league — straight — in front of her.

She heard Norman Gossett's gasp of astonishment and allowed a small smile to cross her lips.

With a shout of joy, Margaret lifted the timber rail ties high in the air, laying them out in the sky with a precision that warmed her heart. She turned toward bare ground and lowered her arms, flicking down them at the last moment.

Chapter One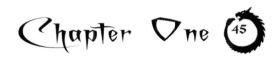

The timbers, laid out like a giant fence in the sky, fell with precision on the ground below.

Shouting with joy, Margaret used her aching arms to raise long lines of rails from the second car and then laid them out on top of the rail ties.

She knelt and bent her head low toward the ground. "Hissia, Hanor, great is your power."

She heard shouts from behind her, shouts of amazement and awe. She rose with a weary sigh then turned toward the approaching men.

But her eyes were on little Ellen as she asked, "How was that?"

"That was beautiful," Ellen Annabelle told her, moving forward to wrap the larger girl in a tight hug. "You are amazing."

"Well, me and the gods," Margaret said, chuckling.

"Always the gods," Ellen agreed.

"Not always," the wispy voice of Hanor corrected her. Ellen's eyes widened and the air god wavered back into sight. He smiled down at her. "Sometimes even gods need to be reminded of their power."

"Like you with your father," Hissia said in agreement.

"We do what we can because the gods love us," Ellen told them solemnly. She waved a hand toward the straight line of track. "We should call this the air line."

"The 'air line'?" Hanor repeated, glancing toward the air goddess.

"That would please us," Hissia agreed. And, with a final nod, the two gods vanished.

Chapter One 47

48 King's Crown

Chapter Two

"There are some places where being a wyvern is a disadvantage," Wymarc said with a long sigh later that day.

"Like in the classroom?" Reedis guessed, nodding in agreement. "I only managed to teach six of the twelve in my class how to lift a cloth bundle."

"Yes, it's hard," Wymarc agreed. Under her breath she added, "Eight."

Reedis' hearing was better than the twin soul wyvern had imagined, for his eyebrows rose in surprise and admiration. "Really? However did you manage —?"

"Centuries of training," Wymarc told him. Reedis' brow fell again in dejection. "Did you tell them the story?"

"What story?" Reedis asked.

"The story of how you built the first airship," Wymarc said.

"I did," Reedis admitted. He smiled in memory. "They were quite amazed, I could tell." His brows creased as he thought to ask, "And you? Did you tell them a story?"

"I did," Wymarc admitted.

"Really?" Reedis prompted.

"I told them the story of how you shot me out of the sky," Wymarc said coldly.

"Oh."

"But I think what helped most was that I identified the natural leaders of the class and challenged them to be the first to learn," Wymarc said, deciding — partly in response to Krea's groans — not to upset the man too much.

"Oh!" Reedis said. "I wish I'd thought of that."

"It took me a century to figure it out," Wymarc admitted.

"Did you have fun?" Nelly asked as she trotted out of her office in response to their voices in the hall.

"I did," Wymarc admitted. "There's something especially *satisfying* about knowing that you've taught."

"There is," Reedis agreed. He beamed at his fiance. "And it's all because of you!"

Nelly blushed and bobbed her head shyly. "Well after dinner, if the two of you would consider teaching *me* what you taught the others —"

"It would be my pleasure," Wymarc told her fondly.

"Mine, too," Reedis added with a grin.

"Mother should be back by then," Nelly said, turning toward the front doors. She frowned. "And Margen, too."

"I suspect that he and Ellen Annabelle are engaged in a little creative air magic right now," Wymarc said.

"Really?" Reedis asked in surprise.

"I saw the track Margaret laid through Korin's Pass," Wymarc said. "I don't doubt that both of them are... *intrigued* with the notion."

"Or jealous," Jarin said with Reedis' voice.

Moira Kendral had never used magic. She didn't need to because she found other people who could do it for her.

"My magic lies elsewhere," she would say when asked. And it did.

Chapter Two

"Hello?" Moira called out at the door. "Is anybody there?" No reply. She tried again, just to be certain, "Hello?"

Nodding to herself, Moira Kendral waved the cabbie away. The cabbie gave her a worried look but flicked the reins and his horse broke into a brisk walk, heading back from the docks toward the center of the town and, hopefully, a new fare.

Moira pushed the door open and peered inside the large building beside the rail station. It was dark. It was dirty.

"Have to do something about that," Moira muttered to herself as she strolled through the doors. She reached into her handbag, felt about and pulled a small bundle from it. "Light!"

The little fire demon responded immediately, rising from her hand and illuminating her way.

"Thank you," Moira said as the little demon led the way further into the darkened chamber. It always pays to be polite to staff, Moira reflected. She'd had the demon for more years than she cared to admit, feeding it at the tavern's fire or bringing it up to the bedroom to sleep in the fireplace.

 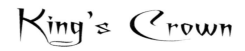 King's Crown

It was a simple creature, wanting little, and Moira treasured it. "Take a look, if you'd like. But no fires, please!"

The fire demon bobbed up and down in front of her in acknowledgement, then sped off. Moira waited a moment, following its path to see what its light disclosed. "Do you see a fireplace?"

The fire demon sped forward, darting into nooks and crannies, its light fading as it was hidden from her and then reappearing a moment later, continuing its journey. When it came to a glassed wall and a door, Moira called, "Wait! Let's go see what's inside, shall we?"

The fire demon bobbed in understanding, and Moira bustled over to it. She found the knob and turned, putting her weight against the door as it stubbornly refused to budge. No good.

"Hmph!" Moira reached into her handbag once more, felt about and pulled another thing from it. It was metal and spiky. She said to it, "See if you can make this door behave, please."

The fire demon flared brighter for a moment in greeting to the earth demon — technically a metal demon — before

Chapter Two 53

resuming its station. Moira pushed the little metal ball to the lock. In a moment, the metal demon had melted into a shape inside the lock and formed a convenient handle which wiggled to Moira invitingly.

"Well done," Moira said as she grasped the protruding end and twisted, like a key in a lock. "Really," she said to herself, "I don't know why people even *bother.*" She slid the door open and gestured for the fire demon to explore while she retrieved the metal demon, which formed once more into a small spiky object and put it back into her purse, telling it, "You did well. I'll let you have a turn in the hearth tonight."

The fire demon hovered over a standing table, and Moira marched over to it. She glanced down, saw a large ledger and smiled to herself.

"There ought to be a lantern somewhere nearby," Moira said suggestively to the fire demon. "Be a dear and see if you can light it."

The demon streaked out of sight, dimmed, and a moment later a larger glow filled the room. Moira moved to take the lantern in her hand and bring in nearer the table. To

King's Crown

"How do immortals do magic?" Angus wondered.

"Much the same way as humans," Rabel said flippantly.

"But humans believe in the gods," Angus said.

"Magic requires understanding the gods, not believing in them," Rabel said. He glanced toward Ibb thoughtfully. "That's right, isn't it?"

"What?" the metal man was staring off toward the warped caravan, apparently deep in thought. "Magic? Yes, we use it. It's not hard."

Rabel nodded, but his expression was reserved.

"How do we fix this, though?" Tracker asked. She glanced to Ibb. "*Can* we fix it?"

"The caravan, restore it to its original shape and purpose?" Ibb asked. Tracker nodded. Ibb shook his head. "No, I don't think we can. It is ruined. We can tear it apart and use the materials again, perhaps."

"Until we can understand how it was destroyed, we'll have little chance of figuring out how to prevent it again," Rabel warned.

"It must have been a god," Tracker said.

Chapter Two

"It wasn't," Rabel said. The others looked to him. "Ophidian said so. There were other gods present, they would have felt it. Not only that, but the place where this occurred was close to a temple, all the gods would have felt it."

"I think it is perhaps better to consider *how* it was done than who did it, for the moment," Ibb said.

"My thinking, too," Rabel agreed. "If we know *how* we can guess who."

"So, once again, the question is: how was it destroyed?" Nestor said. The others glanced toward him and nodded. Then they glanced toward the caravan and frowned.

"Let us assume," Rabel said, "that your Lyric set the spell."

"She wasn't there when the caravan was destroyed," Angus said.

"A spell can be set to cast at a particular time," Rabel said.

"Or a particular set of circumstances," Pallas said. Nestor was always amazed at the way his voice changed when the female ice serpent spoke through it. He was also quite impressed with Pallas' extensive understanding of magic. In

 60  King's Crown

Chapter Three

Nothing! In three days riding, they had seen nothing out of hand. Villages were small, sparse, their inhabitants scared, hidden when they could be, cowed when they were forced to show themselves. Jaweer Elwes was pleased to take their tribute — it saved on their supplies — but disturbed by the poor lands around them.

At night the birdmen rose and allowed themselves to be catapulted into the sky where they turned into their eagle forms, screeched defiance, and disappeared into the darkness. When they returned and changed back into their human shape, it was always the same: nothing to report. At least not to the captain.

Gamdan Ikar was the leader and elder of the two. The other was Jaden Ostan, who nursed his jaw and shot dark looks at his leader when he thought the other wouldn't notice. Captain Elwes would not have turned his back on either of them.

They were looking for impossible things, things that no longer existed. Centaurs, and… what were *hexine?* But the Grand Duke had sent him on a mission and Captain Elwes knew the price of failure.

He spotted a hill rising in the distance and pointed it out to his lieutenant. "The sun will set soon enough, let's head there so that our feathered friends may have an easy launch."

"Alain Casman, well met," a voice spoke from behind him. Alain jumped and turned. There had been no one behind him the moment before. And now — now there were four. All girls. Alain took a second look and wondered if he should correct himself — perhaps there were three girls and one woman. Or…

She's here! Seena cried in triumph. *You must bow to her, she's a goddess!*

Alain's eyes widened, and he said, "You're a goddess?" He had only a moment to take in her amused expression before he fell to his knees. "How may I serve you?"

King's Crown

Careful! Seena warned. The hexine had become very comfortable talking to Alain even as the others — Mayse and Janzie — smouldered with resentment. His sister — thank goodness! — had calmed the two centaurs down, reminding them that his ancestry made him at least a duke.

"First, stand up," the goddess ordered. Alain rose quickly to his feet. He glanced at the other three — one was lying on the ground, asleep or drugged.

Alain's brows creased, and he demanded, "What have you done with her?" Before anyone could respond, Alain darted to the girl and put a hand to her head.

You have the gift of your forebears, Seena said in amazement.

Alain ignored her, concentrating on the unconscious girl. He took a deep breath, closed his eyes and probed. A moment later he stood up and turned to the goddess. "What happened?"

"Who *is* he?" the dark girl spoke up, giving Alain a fierce look.

"Tell me, youngling, what do you think happened?" the goddess asked.

Chapter Three

"I am Alain Casman," he said with a bow to the goddess, "just recently arrived from the north with my sister."

"Your father was Pier Casman, Grand Duke of the Jasram Plain," the goddess said. "Your mother — " her brow creased as she looked thoughtfully at Alain "-- you do not know about your mother."

"My sister is a centaur," Alain said. He bowed low and, when he rose, said, "Might I know your name, fair goddess?"

"I am Kahlas."

The goddess of the Moon, of dreams, mother of the centaurs, the hexine, and many others, Leetar informed him.

Kahlas laughed, a loud pleasant chuckle from deep in her chest. She waved a hand toward the hexine. "And I see you are with child!"

Indeed, oh wise one! Seena replied.

Kahlas turned her gaze back to Alain and smiled. "For the others," she said, waving a hand toward the two girls standing and the unconscious one on the ground, "kindly relay what she said."

Alain glanced at the newcomers. The oldest was the dark-eyed girl. Next eldest was the girl on the ground. But

 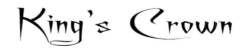

both seemed dimmer than the third girl. His eyes narrowed as if blinded and his jaw gaped as he blurted, "There are *two* of you!"

The girl's eyes widened in surprise, and she glanced toward Kahlas in question.

"Alain!" Lisette called, running over. "Mayze says — " she broke off as she saw the others.

"Lisette, bow to the goddess!" Alain called urgently to her. Lisette stopped in her tracks, caught herself, and dipped in an elegant curtsy.

"Hello, mother," she said to the goddess. "I am Lisette Marie."

Kahlas eyed her and smiled. "I did not make you," she said, "but I greet you, daughter."

"Ellen Annabelle made me," Lisette said. "After I fell from the cliff high above."

"I know," Kahlas said. She waved a hand to the others behind her. "These are Bethany Margiss — a wyvern — Chandra her rider, and Barbara Garrett who is under my case." Her eyes cut to Alain in a strange look.

"What happened to her, may I ask?" Alain said.

Chapter Three 69

"What do you think?" Kahlas asked.

"Her mind was hurt more than her body," Alain said instantly. He could not quite understand how he knew that.

Because you are the same, Leetar spoke up in his mind.

"Can she hear the hexine?" Alain asked Kahlas.

The goddess shook her head. "Her gift is with air; she is a mage."

"I see," Alain said, trying to hide the fact that he most certainly did *not* see.

"My magic is earth magic," Chandra spoke up, smiling at Lisette Marie and giving Alain a cautious look.

"May I tell him?" Margiss asked the goddess. Kahlas smiled and nodded. Margiss took a breath and said, "Our magic is healing, mostly of the mind, but we're new and don't know much."

"What can I do for you?" Alain asked the goddess. "You should know that I'm new here myself and —"

"Alain Casman! Just what do you — " Mayse's voice broke off as she came storming up to them. She stopped, looked at the newcomers, bristled at their presence and

 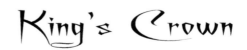 King's Crown

started to speak angrily when Alain cut her off with an upraised hand.

"Mayse, may I make you known to the goddess Kahlas?"

"You!" Mayse said, pointing to Kahlas. Suddenly she was crying, bawling, her face wet with tears. "Do you know how often we… we.."

Kahlas moved and grabbed the woman in her arms, hugging her tightly and pulling her head against her shoulder. "I know dear, I watched, and I heard, but I had to wait until the time was right."

Mayse pulled her head off the goddess' shoulder and wiped her tears. "And is it?"

"It is," Kahlas told her. "Now comes your time to decide. You and Janzie both."

"What's to decide?" Mayse said, drawing herself straight and then bowing deeply to the goddess.

"First the healing, then the war," Kahlas warned her.

"War?" Alain said.

"Yes," Kahlas said, turning to smile at him. "You *do* want your crown back, don't you?"

Chapter Three ⟨71⟩

"It's not the crown," Alain told her firmly. "It's the people."

"Which is why, Your Highness, you will need your crown," Kahlas said.

"I don't know how to be a good ruler," Alain confessed, his misery apparent.

Which is why you'll need to learn, Leetar told him.

"I don't like it," Jacques Martel said sourly to Mage Tirpin as they stood beside their lamed, tired horses, eyeing a farmhouse in the distance. Snow was coming down steadily and it was hard to realize that it was still some hours before sunset. "There should be activity, some lights on — something!"

"Our horses are lame, our bellies are growling, we should approach the house and at least *see* what we can learn," Tirpin growled in reply.

"But if they're poor, they'll be able to do nothing for us," Martel protested.

"So?"

"So, my friend," Martel said in a biting tone, "if they are too poor to help us, they are perhaps desperate enough to sell information."

Tirpin frowned. "About us?"

Martel nodded.

"We can deal with that," Tirpin said. He started forward and turned around when Martel didn't follow. Walking backwards, Tirpin called, "Do you want to starve?"

With an irritated curse, the former airship captain grabbed the reins of the two lamed horses and tugged them into a walk.

Tirpin waited until the other caught up and then fell into step beside him. "Consider this," Tirpin offered diplomatically, pointing to the snow-filled sky above them, "if we still had the airship, we'd be *much* colder up there."

"If we still had an airship," Martel replied sourly, "we'd be *there* by now!"

"It will take us at least ten days, more likely two weeks to reach the border," Michael Armand, formerly general of

the Sorian army, said to his companion as they rode westward through the falling snow.

"Yes," Ingam Oliver, mage and former chief of staff of the Sorian Army, agreed blandly. "And then we shall have to make some decisions."

"Oh?"

"Do we go north to Hjalvik or south to Nikjal?" Ingam asked. He pronounced the letter 'j' as a 'y' in the tradition of Vinik — actually the tradition of both Vinik and South Vinik, the two sundered kingdoms to the west. So Hjalvik was 'hee-yal-vik' and Nikjal was pronounced 'Neek-yal.'

"Hjalvik if we want to warn them, Nikjal if we want to join?" Michael Armand guessed.

"Say rather that Hjalvik will be more direct, but going to Nikjal might be more certain," Oliver said.

"Of course, the Emperor might decide that we need to lose weight," Armand said dryly, pointing a hand to his head for example.

Oliver chuckled. "Which is why it might be smarter to go to Hjalvik and see how things stand."

King's Crown

"We have time," Armand agreed. "I can't imagine King Markel planning an attack until the spring thaw at the earliest."

"But you didn't expect him to attack us in the winter," Oliver said. "It could be that his generals and mages have more surprises prepared."

"In which case our lives will be short," Michael Armand said. He waved a hand to the path ahead. "For now, we should keep going to the Pinch. We'll have plenty of time to think along the way."

"What do we do now?" Margaret asked Ellen Annabelle and Peter Hewlitt when she'd finished laying the track. The railcrew were busy hammering in the rail ties and would be busy for the rest of the day.

"We should go back to Kingsford," Thomas Walpish said. Skara Ningan nodded fervently beside him.

"But after?" Margaret asked. "The rail line here and the one from Korin's Pass — what about them?"

Chapter Three 75

"I see your point," Hewlitt said, pursing his lips. He glanced to mage Margen and waved a hand at the laid tracks. "Could you do that?"

Margen shook his head and told Margaret Waters, "I have not such skill with air." Honestly, he added, "I doubt many others do."

"Barbara was good," Matt Evans chimed in loyally. Beside him, Freddie Fennimore nodded in agreement.

"And we have to consider you too," Hewlitt told the two youths.

"Moira, with the other team, she's pretty good," Margaret said. "They get the job done."

"Let us go back and see how things fare at the school," Margen said. He turned to Ellen Annabelle and waved a hand toward Matt and Freddie. "Could you make two trips so that we can bring these two with us?"

"No, she cannot," Margaret said firmly. The others turned to her. "She's done enough already this day and is more tired than she's willing to admit."

"She's right," Annabelle said with Ellen's voice. "Ellen would never admit it but…"

 King's Crown

"Perhaps the mage and I could stay here the night," Peter suggested. "And if you couldn't return in the morning, perhaps Jarin Reedis would do us the favor?"

"Or you could take the train back to the capital," Margaret suggested. "And bring the railcrew with you." She nodded toward the workers in the distance. "In the morning, when they're done."

"I have no right to dictate —" Hewlitt began cautiously.

"Are you not a member of the King's court?" Thomas Walpish demanded. "And does that not give you power when none other is present?"

Hewlitt gave the ghost a thoughtful look.

"Our mission is to protect Ellen Annabelle," Skara added in agreement. She glanced fondly at the girl. "And she needs food, rest, and a chance to wind down."

"Very well," Hewlitt said. "Mage Margen, does this plan suit you?"

"I do believe, spymaster, that you had something you wished to discuss with me," Margan said in oblique agreement.

Chapter Three 77

Hewlitt smiled and looked much, much younger than he had moments before. "Indeed, I do!"

Chapter Four

"It might be a good idea not to mention us to Mrs. Kendral," Thomas Walpish said as he and Skara took guard positions around Margaret and Ellen Annabelle.

"She might surprise you," Annabelle said.

"But, all the same…" Skara said.

"I think they're right," Margaret said, nodding toward Ellen Annabelle. "It might frighten her out of her wits."

"Very well," Ellen said reluctantly. She raised her eyes to Margaret. "But I think you may be wrong about the innkeeper's wife."

They climbed the stairs leading into the school. Dusk had fallen, the last rays of the sun were glinting off the sea in the west. The interior of the school was well lit, and it was warm inside.

"I never knew this existed," Margaret said, eyeing the hall with interest.

"It's new," Thomas Walpish said. Skara eyed him warningly and he gave her an apologetic look.

"Hello!" Ellen yelled. "Jarin! Nelly! We're back!"

"We're in here!" a voice none of them recognized called back. "In the kitchen, come along, we've got leftovers!"

Ellen picked up her pace and was matched by Margaret at her side and Thomas and Skara — invisibly — at front and rear.

The room was just around the corner and not too large. A woman with her back to them was stirring a pot. Jarin Reedis and Nelly Kendral sat at a small table, smiling lovingly at each other. In front of them were two empty bowls. The smell from the pot on the stove revealed that they had previously held a marvelous spicy stew.

"Where's Margen?" Reedis asked as the party entered the room. He saw Thomas point at himself and wave his hand in warning. "And Hewlitt?"

"They stayed behind," Margaret said. "They're going to take the train back here in the morning."

"Oh? Sensible," Reedis allowed. "Are they bringing the two youngsters back with them?"

King's Crown

"Probably," Annabelle said with Ellen's voice.

"Good idea," the woman at the stove said. She turned and took in the two people she saw, her lips pursing as she took in Ellen Annabelle, then changing again when her eyes caught sight of Margaret. She grabbed a kitchen towel and wiped her hands, moving forward with her right hand extended to the smallest person in the room. "I'm Moira Kendral, Nelly's mother."

"We're pleased to meet you, ma'am," Annabelle said with Ellen's voice. Moira's eyes widened and then she glanced to her own daughter. "Nelly was right, you can tell the difference!"

"I'm Margaret Waters," the taller girl said, reaching to shake Mrs. Kendral's hand. She glanced past her to the pot on the stove. "Can I serve?"

"No, you'll do nothing of the sort," Mrs. Kendral said with a sniff. "Take those seats and I'll get you something immediately." She shot a sharp glance toward her daughter, and blushing, Nelly rose to help her.

In short order, the newcomers were seated with steaming bowls of stew in front of them.

Chapter Four 81

"This looks marvelous!" Ellen exclaimed, diving in.

Mrs. Kendral tutted and said, "Did you not want to thank the gods first?"

"No," Ellen said, wolfing down her food, "they've done nothing for me."

"You've all the manners of an urchin!" Mrs. Kendral exclaimed.

"That's because she was," Annabelle said, taking control of Ellen's voice. "She would have died had it not been for Rabel."

"Rabel?" Mrs. Kendral said. "The smith?"

"Yes," Annabelle said. "He took her in."

"After his daughter turned into a wyvern?"

"After he was thrown in the jail," Ellen said, "and left to die."

"Oh!" Mrs. Kendral said in a much smaller voice. She turned back to the stove, grabbed some mugs from the shelf to the side and poured two cups of hot tea. "Here, there's honey on the table," she said as she served the two girls.

"Thank you," Ellen said, using both hands to grab the mug.

Babette Collet shivered in the cold. Night had fully fallen and there was nothing to keep her warm save the jacket that one prisoner had loaned her.

"You must wait until it is dark," Amuir had told her. "The power needed is in the dark."

Babette had nodded in understanding. The spell was simple, not too different from the one that had pulled her to Queen Airivik's burial mound — the place where she'd found the ghost of her murdered father.

"Look for one who is very drunk and very troubled," General Dartan had added. "Someone who feels guilt."

Babette had nodded once again.

Now, she stood huddled in the shadows outside a tavern which was packed with Kingsland soldiers. She'd spotted an officer going inside, pulled by his men, and had decided that he would be the one.

So she waited. And waited. The noise changed, there was an exclamation from inside and shouting and then the officer

Chapter Four 83

burst out of the doors, pulled up his collar and stormed off into the night.

Babette followed.

"Where's Krea?" Ellen asked as she sat back from the table, her half-empty mug in one hand and an empty bowl in front of her.

"Right here," Krea Wymarc said, coming into view from the hallway. She turned and waved a hand toward two girls behind her. "These ladies had some extra questions for me."

The two girls giggled, bobbed their heads nervously, and sped away.

"There's still some stew," Mrs. Kendral told her, gesturing her toward the table. "I can warm up some water for tea."

"Thank you," Krea said. She made a motioning hand behind her back. "And for Drake, too?"

"Drake?" Mrs. Kendral said.

A dark-haired lad ducked his head in the doorway behind Krea.

"My bodyguard when I'm human, rider when I'm a wyvern," Krea said.

Mrs. Kendral's eyebrows rose, and she turned to Jarin Reedis. "Is this the same for dragons, then?"

"It is," Reedis answered. He nodded toward Nelly. "The rider of a dragon or wyvern is security if anything happens to the mortal half of the twin soul."

"The mortal half?" Mrs. Kendral repeated. "That would be you."

"Yes," Reedis said. He gestured toward Nelly, who blushed. "I've asked Nelly if she'd accept the honor."

"And I've agreed," Nelly said, smiling back at him.

"Of course, we hope that nothing happens to either," Jarin said with Reedis' voice. "And I argued with both of them but... Reedis presented a powerful argument."

Nelly rose from the table and gestured for Krea Wymarc to take her place. Seeing this, Reedis also rose and waved Drake into his chair.

"I suppose if anything were to happen to you," Mrs. Kendral said, "it would be best to have the two who have the most hurt able to console each other."

Chapter Four

"That was my thought, also," Reedis allowed. He bowed to her and grabbed Nelly's hand. "And now, if you will all forgive us, I have promised my intended some lessons on magic."

Nelly squeezed his hand and beamed with delight, turning and dragging him out of the room.

"Lessons!" Annabelle chortled.

Mrs. Kendral waved her ladle toward the twin soul. "You're too young to be talking that way!"

"Actually," Annabelle replied, "*I'm* not."

"Then she is," Mrs. Kendral responded immediately.

"Ugh!" Ellen said, catching on. "Although, Mrs. Kendral, I really do believe that Reedis means lessons, as in magic."

"He was the one who taught me balloon magic," Annabelle said in agreement.

"And the academy is named after him," Krea Wymarc added. "It's only fitting that the principal know the magic."

"We should clean up," Ellen Annabelle said, rising from her seat. Margaret joined her and the two put their dishes into the sink.

"Thank you, I appreciate that," Mrs. Kendral said.

"And how was your day?" Margaret asked. She sounded tired and worn out. Mrs. Kendral shot her a worried look.

"Not, no doubt, as tiring as yours, but intriguing," Mrs. Kendral replied. "I took a moment to examine your father's books."

"Books?" Margaret said. "Magic books?"

"In a way, yes," Mrs. Kendral said. "I went over his business records."

"And what did you find?" Drake asked, looking up from his stew.

"I think I'd best wait until I can talk with Mr. Hewlitt."

"Well, *that's* done," Crown Prince Sarsal muttered to himself as he closed the door to his royal chamber and threw off the ornately embroidered tunic that he'd been forced to wear throughout the damned proceedings. As it fell to the floor, he frowned, bent and picked it up, placing it on the back of one of the lounge chairs in his anteroom. "At least until tomorrow."

Ah, yes, tomorrow! The true coronation. He had survived the dress rehearsal, he'd probably survive the real thing.

"I'll survive," he muttered to himself, his lips curving upwards. "And then there'll be refreshments."

"Talking to oneself, even in one's own quarters, is never wise," a voice spoke from the shadows. "You never know who might be listening."

"Or, you might, if you're someone like myself who has trained from birth, have used a spell to sheath the room in a silence spell," Sarsal replied. He turned hooded eyes toward the speaker. "Did you get it?"

"I did," the woman replied, stepping out of the shadows. She was, if anything, prettier than her sister. Certainly she was smarter.

"And the plans?"

"As you desire, my prince," Melodie Gregory said, smiling at him. She reached up and moved to release the robe that was covering her nightgown. It slipped off. The nightgown underneath was thin and, with the light behind it, revealing.

"I desire much," Crown Prince Sarsal said. He gestured her toward the bed in the far room, pulling off his own shirt as he walked through the door.

She giggled as he grabbed her and threw her on the bed. She really was *much* prettier than Matilda.

"Quiet, wench," he said mockingly. "Have some respect for the dead."

The girl shook her head. "I know full well, Your Highness, that this is *not* the room in which my sister died. You changed quarters immediately afterwards."

"I didn't mean her," Sarsal said, unlacing his shoes and throwing them off. He rose to unhitch his trousers and threw them off, turning to her with a smile. "I mean those about to die."

"Oh, them!" Melodie snorted. "I'll stand beside you as they gasp their last, and I'll smile as they die."

"That's my girl," Sarsal said, turning back to the bed and throwing himself at her.

A long time later, as they languished beside each other, he said to her, "This time tomorrow, you'll be queen."

Chapter Four 89

"What is the meaning of this?" Emperor Maximilian Kursk roared as the doors to his royal throne room burst open and two lifeless forms flew to land at his feet.

"It's an introduction," a man's voice came in reply. A figure lurched through the doors, a brilliant staff in one hand and the ear of a small child in the other. The child was still attached to the ear and squirming miserably. "A proof of power, as it were." The man threw the child by her ear as she skidded across the long floor of the throne room to come to rest near the two bodies. "Surely you recognize my calling card?"

"Guards!" Maximilian roared. His guards were already in motion — and then they weren't, standing frozen in mid-stride.

The man stopped and glowered at the Emperor. "I *said*, surely you recognize my calling card?" The girl was hunched over, her hands to her face, tears streaming endlessly. The man growled at her, "Stop snivelling." The girl flinched as if struck and fell in a heap.

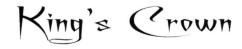

"Who are you?" Emperor Maximilian of Vinik demanded.

"I'm your new mage," the man said with a crooked smile. He pointed his staff toward the larger of the two bodies on the floor. "I bested your last one and his apprentice." He frowned. "A son, I believe. Though not much of a son." He waved his staff toward the hunched girl. "That's his daughter, too. I shall take her in his stead."

The girl on the floor flinched at those words.

The man said confidentially, "I've had a great deal of success in raising children, you know."

"You are a mage," Maximilian decided. He glanced down at the two corpses in front of him. "And you think defeating my best mage gives you his position?"

"I could defeat the rest of them, but who would do the scut work then?" the man replied. "I like having apprentices."

"Who are you?"

"You may call me the Magemaster," the man replied. "I come bearing glorious news: soon you will be king."

"I am an Emperor!" Maximilian shouted. "Why would I want to be king?"

Chapter Four

"You are emperor of one small slice of land," the Magemaster replied. "I am sent to offer you the whole land."

"South Vinik?" Maximilian guessed, licking his lips in anticipation.

"South Vinik, Soria, Kingsland, Palu — those are just names," the Magemaster replied. He caught the Emperor's eyes in his gaze. "I'm talking about Cuiyival. The entire continent." He shrugged. "Maybe more, if you please my master."

"Your master?"

"Often he is called the three-headed god," the Magemaster told him. "I'm sure you'll be happy to serve him."

"You must rest," mage Margen told Peter Hewlitt. "Magic is work and, like all work, unused muscles get the most tired and need the greatest rest."

"But I hardly did anything," Hewlitt said.

Margen grunted and pointed to the fireplace. "We need a fire."

King's Crown

Hewlitt's brow furrowed. "How?"

"Imagine the heat, the light," Margen told him. "And then make it be so."

"A huge roaring fire?"

"No," Margen said, laughing, "just a spark is all that's needed."

"Right," Hewlitt said, chagrined.

A moment later a small spark appeared, grew brighter, dimmed, and died.

"Try it again," Margen said.

"Very well," Hewlitt said. He took a deep breath and let it out slowly. As he did, the spark returned, grew brighter — and then a small flame appeared. Slowly it grew, growing to fill the fireplace.

"Good magic always begins small," Margen told him. "And a smart man uses just enough of it to do his will."

"I see," Hewlitt said, staring proudly into the fire. "It's much like spying."

"How so?"

Chapter Four 93

"One only need learn enough to know something," Hewlitt said. "And usually all it takes is a simple question and a willing ear."

"Huh," Margen grunted. "I'd never thought of it that way."

"Most people think it requires threats, bribes, and treachery," Hewlitt said in agreement. "But often I learn the most by being quiet and listening honestly."

"Well, magic is *not* like that," Margen said. "It requires thought, study, and preparation." He stood and threw back the covers of the small bed nearest the fire. He gestured toward Hewlitt and the farther bed, the one nearest the window. "You can have that one."

Hewlitt nodded and went to the further bed, removed his boots and got under the inadequate blankets. "I think I shall like magic," Hewlitt said.

"Really?"

"Just like spying, it requires thought, study, and preparation," Hewlitt replied lightly.

"Hmph!"

 94  King's Crown

Chapter Five

"The wind is picking up, it's off our stern," Captain Fawcett said as Major Lewis came up on deck in the early morning. The airship *Wasp* was moving fast over the ground below.

"That's good?" Lewis guessed from the captain's cheerful tone.

"We might see Korin's Pass by this afternoon."

"Good, can't wait to get there," Lewis said.

"And if we don't it'll be a hard slog," Fawcett added more somberly. "We're almost out of coal."

"There's plenty of wood here to burn if we need it," Lewis said, eyeing the ship's timbers critically.

"It won't come to that," Captain Fawcett said.

"The king needs his treasure, captain," Lewis reminded him. "I'll do what it takes."

"She did *that?*" a young lad's voice exclaimed loudly in the morning air. "Why on Earth did you let her?"

"I was unconscious at the time, I didn't have any say in it," a girl's voice replied.

"Ahoy the gates!" a child's voice — a girl's — piped up.

"We come to offer help," a man's voice added. "Please send for Queen Diam and tell her that Ellen Annabelle and Jarin Reedis have come to redeem Chandra's word!"

From out of the ruins of the gate, a small form stepped forward. "Oh, it's you!" the figure said, his voice deeper than his height. "It's about time!"

"We had some distractions along the way," Jarin Reedis said with a delicate cough.

"Is that Granno?" Ellen asked.

"Ellen?" Granno replied, stepping into sight. "I might have known."

"Chandra's gone with Kahlas, so Freddie here is going to redeem her word," the small girl gestured to a taller lad, who nodded, eyes wide with amazement to the zwerg bodyguard.

King's Crown

"Why aren't you with Her Majesty?" Jarin Reedis asked.

"She's got more than one bodyguard," Granno grumbled. "And she asked me to see what could be done for this entrance."

"It is *rather* obvious at the moment," Freddie, the lad who had spoken first, agreed. He glanced toward a young woman and said, "Remind me never to get your sister angry."

"I remind everyone never to get Chandra angry," Margaret Waters assured him. She gestured toward the ruined gates and the crack splitting the entrance. "Can you fix it?"

Freddie gave her a dubious look in reply. "I've never seen such destruction."

"We could ask Mage Margen," Ellen Annabelle suggested evenly.

Freddie Fenimore's face clouded, and he shook his head. "Let me try, first." He nodded toward Granno. "How would you like me to fix it?"

"We need it buried, hidden, so no one can ever find it again," Granno told him.

"But how will you get out again?" Margaret asked worriedly.

Chapter Five

Granno brought a finger to the side of his nose and said slyly, "Best you not know, miss."

"The zwerg like to keep their entrances hidden," Jarin explained. "There are too many humans hoping to steal their gold."

"You skytouchers are always tearing things up," Granno said.

Margaret stiffened in hurt. "Chandra was just trying to help me —"

Granno cut her off with a raised hand. "I wasn't talking about your sister, nor these others —" he waved his hand to include Ellen Annabelle and Jarin Reedis "-- neither of them have the gold sickness. But there've been others."

"So how far in do you wish us to bury this?" Jarin Reedis asked. "And are there any zwerg nearby that might need to be warned?"

"I'm the only one here," Granno said. "I was just trying to figure how best —"

The ground started shaking. Everyone turned to see that Freddie was kneeling down on one knee, his right hand resting on the ground, his brow taut with concentration. "I

can do this," he said as the others looked at him. To Granno, he added, "Do you need to go inside or do you have another way?"

"Stop!" Granno barked. The ground stopped shaking. "First, lad, we're going to see what the queen desires."

"How will she know she's needed?" Margaret asked.

"I suspect the ground shaking will catch her attention," Jarin Reedis said with a small smile. "In the meantime, Granno, may I make you known to my fiance, the mage and teacher, Nelly Kendral?" He gestured to the woman clutching his arm tightly.

Granno bowed toward Nelly. "Congratulations, miss!" To Jarin he said, "How did you manage to get so lucky?"

"We'd met before I'd gone to the bitter north in the *Spite*," Reedis explained. "When I returned, I found that Nelly had set up a school of magic in my memory."

"Well, I'm thrilled for the both of you," Granno said enthusiastically. He bobbed his head toward Nelly. "Jarin Reedis are beloved in our kingdom, miss."

"They even allow me to nest in their gold," Jarin added.

 Chapter Five ⟨99⟩

"Well, now, Mister Jarin, I'm not sure that's the sort of thing we like others to know," Granno said in a soft, warning tone.

"Granno, she's going to be my wife!" Reedis said. "And she's agreed to be our rider."

"Rider?" Granno said, brows rising. "You mean, in case —"

"Exactly," Reedis said. He patted Nelly's hand. "If anything happens to me, I'll at least have the knowledge that she and Jarin will be safe."

"And nothing had better happen to you!" Nelly told him fiercely.

"I really don't understand why shaman Riess wasn't available," King Markel muttered as he and his new queen gathered before the doors to the royal temple.

"He wasn't feeling well, Your Majesty," Crown Prince Sarsal told him. "He sends his regrets, and he personally assured me that Meister Semple would be more than capable as his substitute."

"But this Meister Semple wasn't the one who crowned your father, was he?" Markel asked waspishly. He glanced toward Rassa. "Won't this cause talk?"

"If people talk, dear, we shall deal with it," Queen Rassa assured, patting his arm.

"In any case, Your Majesties, it's time," first minister Mannevy said as the guards swung open the huge double doors that led into the royal temple.

The royal trumpeters began their coronation processional. King Markel gave his new queen a wintry smile, raised a hand for hers and, together, the two started their royal progress down the aisle surrounded by nobles, statues of gods, and the whole of the new kingdom's royalty.

"No sign of General Armand?" General Gergen asked, popping up beside Mannevy's side.

"What?" Mannevy asked, distracted by the question from his attentive gaze on the king and queen as they made their stately way to the end of their walk and turned to face the approving roar of the crowd. Of course, the crowd was *paid* to roar approvingly, but Mannevy was the only one who knew that. He and Crown Prince Sarsal, of course. The young

Chapter Five

lad was quite obsequious and helpful. Mannevy appreciated that.

"What?" he asked again.

"General Armand," General Gergen said, his tone frosty. "I've been trying to find out who he's picked to lead the cavalry all day and I can't find him."

"He's in there, somewhere," Mannevy said, absently pointing to the thronging crowd in the temple. "Doubtless you'll find him later at the celebration."

"I suppose," Gergen said doubtfully. He turned away and then turned back. "And that's another thing —"

"Yes?" Mannevy interrupted, turning his gaze to the general.

"How are we going to house all the troops?" Gergen asked. "There can't be a hall large enough for the men of *both* armies."

"No," Mannevy agreed, "there isn't. You and your troops will be at one hall, Armand and his men in another."

Gergen gave him a look.

"It was the best we could do," Mannevy said. "If it hadn't been for Prince Sarsal, you'd all be eating in the stables."

"Sarsal found us a place?"

"Two places," Mannevy corrected absently. "Perhaps you should head there now."

"Not until I see them properly crowned," Gergen said.

"Of course," Mannevy agreed, turning his gaze back to the far end of the temple where Meister Semple was speaking inaudibly.

"I hope he doesn't make a mess of things," Gergen muttered, eyeing the coronation dubiously. "He's not their regular man, is he?"

"The other one is ill," Mannevy agreed absently. "But we only need this one for the next few minutes. When he's done, we'll be feasting for the rest of the day." He started forward, turning back to say to Gergen, "If you'll excuse me, this is a day I have awaited for a long time."

Gergen nodded and waved him away.

First minister Mannevy moved forward by way of the outside aisle, behind the nobles to the top of the temple. Shaman Semple, with white-frosted hair and eyebrows, looked none too steady as he shuffled forward to stand before and between Markel and Rassa.

Chapter Five 103

Mannevy moved out of the shadows and took a place to the left of the queen, close enough to hear and beam encouragingly. But at the first words from the shaman, his face fell.

"Today, we ahr heah to unite these two souls in joyous harmony," the shaman said in a languid drawl, solemnly turning his head from Rassa to Markel and back again. "The sanctity of marriage brings us closer to the gods."

"The coronation," Mannevy hissed. "They're here for the coronation!"

"Not the wedding?" shaman Semple asked, eyes going wide. He licked his lips. "But I thought — I thought —"

"That, too," Mannevy said, moving closer to the raised dais. "The marriage, then the coronation."

"There ahr rings?" Semple asked seriously despite his drawl.

"Your Majesty, the rings," Mannevy said, nodding toward King Markel. Markel felt inside his rich cloak and pulled forth two rings, passing one to Rassa whose expression was beyond rage.

King's Crown

"With these rings, you exchange your pledges," Semple said, nodding to Markel who placed the ring on Rassa's finger. Rassa dimpled and curtsied before moving forward to place Markel's ring on his finger.

"Declare them man and wife," Mannevy urged, waving angrily at the shaman, "and then get on with the coronation?"

"Have you the crowns?" Semple asked Mannevy. With a strangled groan, Mannevy waved to the two crowns, fully visible, placed on the table behind the shaman. Semple turned at his urging and jerked in surprise when he spied them. "Good, then we should proceed."

"Man and wife!" Mannevy hissed to the shaman in reminder.

"Man and wife?" Semple repeated blankly, clearly thrown by the course of events.

"That'll do," Rassa growled, her eyes hooding her anger. "Get on with the coronation."

Semple nodded and turned back to pick up the King's crown.

Chapter Five 105

"The Queen *first*," Mannevy growled at the man in frustration. He'd made it very clear to the shaman that the queen, as the former queen of Soria, must be crowned first.

Semple's eyes widened, and he nodded jerkily, moving forward and placing the King's crown on Queen Rassa's head. The crown, hastily re-sized the day before, slipped over Rassa's eyes.

"The *other* crown," Mannevy said with a groan.

Semple realized his mistake, pulled off the king's crown, moved and placed it on King Markel's head as though he were a hatstand and retrieved the queen's crown from the table.

"With this crown, receive the fealty of all Soria," Semple said, lowering the crown on Queen Rassa's head. He turned to the assembly and called out, "All rise for Queen Rassa!"

Mannevy stifled a groan: the shaman was supposed to call the assembly to their feet *after* King Markel had been crowned. Markel caught Mannevy's eyes with a baleful look; the first minister took a deep breath and let it out slowly, nodding to direct his king's attention back to the shaman.

  King's Crown

"And now, *me*, if you would," Markel said in icy tones to the shaman.

"But you have already got your crown!" Semple said in purest confusion.

"Declare him king and oath-holder!" Mannevy ordered the shaman.

Semple looked at him as if seeing him for the first time, recovered and raised his arms above Markel.

"All rise for the new King of Sowia and give him fealty!" Shaman Semple called.

The assembly, already on their feet, looked at each other in confusion, trying to decide on their course of action.

"Long live the King!" Mannevy shouted. "Long live King Markel and Queen Rassa!"

"Long live the King!" the assembly dutifully bellowed back. Mannevy turned and gestured to the choir standing behind him. Several children in its midst were openly laughing. He glared at them and signalled the choirmaster to begin the recessional. The choir master nodded in understanding, raised his arms, and the choir sang the Sorian anthem.

The crowd turned and slowly filed out of the temple.

Chapter Five 107

Rassa and Markel stood before them, beaming at each other with huge grins on their faces and holding hands.

"Well," Shaman Semple said as he tottered over to Mannevy, "I think that went rahteh well."

"What's that noise?" Captain Welless called from his front office. "I say, Mr. Beck, what's that rumbling?"

"Outside!" Hamo Beck roared, putting action to his words, charging out of his inner office and dragging the Kingsland captain after him. "It is an earthquake!"

The booming sound dropped off just as the same time as the ground rippled up and down, causing buildings to shake and groan under the stresses.

Captain Welless looked around, turned southward and stared. "Something to do with your kin?" Welless asked, his brow creased. "Should we be worried?"

"No," Hamo Beck said after a moment. "I believe that was the gate being closed."

"I heard no explosion," Captain Welless said.

King's Crown

"No, that was magic," Hamo said in agreement. He gave the captain a wry look. "I suspect that perhaps our mage friends repaid the zwerg for their aid."

"Hmph," Welless said, looking thoughtful. He turned to Beck. "They might have warned us."

"They are rather impulsive and my kinsfolk were probably eager for the protection," Beck replied.

"Well, yes, I could understand that," Welless agreed. "Don't want every greedy gold hunter tracking them down." He pointed to the rising cloud of dust and added thoughtfully, "Though that might be hard to explain."

"Every mage in a hundred miles will have felt it," Beck said.

"Every *person* in a hundred miles will have felt *and* heard it," Welless corrected. He shrugged. "Well, there's nothing I can do about it."

"Call it an earthquake when asked," Hamo Beck suggested lightly.

"Oh, *that* was obvious!" Welless exclaimed. He turned back to their office and gestured for the mayor to precede him. "Let us hope we have no more excitement in the day."

Chapter Five 109

"I haven't really had much chance to travel on the train," Mage Margen said to Peter Hewlitt as the train chugged steadily northwards.

Hewlitt sketched a quick smile. "I can well imagine."

"And how long until we reach the capital?"

Hewlitt looked up thoughtfully before answering, "About two hours."

"Hmm," Margen was clearly not impressed with the train's speed.

"We're pulling five cars," Hewlitt replied, "one with passengers and four with goods." He smiled at the mage. "That's about forty tons of goods."

"Hmm," and this time Margen's tone was entirely different, "*that's* something no mage would consider."

"Which is why I like the trains," Hewlitt agreed.

"I see," Margen said. He sat back for a moment, enjoying the scenery outside their window and the way it rushed by them. "Didn't you say you wanted to talk with me, earlier?"

Hewlitt smiled once more and nodded. "Indeed, I do."

 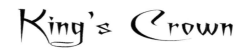

"Something to do with your position and magic, I imagine."

"Not *quite*," Peter Hewlitt told him. "I was thinking more in terms of finance and profit."

"Please don't tell me you want to talk about turning lead into gold," Margen groaned.

"Nothing of the sort," Hewlitt said. "Gold is a nice metal and I respect it but I'm more... direct in my thinking: I want what it can buy and the power that comes with it."

"Hmm."

"I also want to help the magic community," Hewlitt said.

"Give yourself a good year of study and you'll be a mage yourself," Margen said, giving the spymaster a look of approval. "You're quite the study."

"Thank you," Hewlitt replied. "But I was thinking of city folk and the common man."

"City folk are not that common," Margen said with a sniff.

"But they are becoming more so," Hewlitt said. "We will always need food and those who harvest it but we have been

Chapter Five

moving for many centuries towards clusters of people. Those clusters have become the centers of trade, of commerce, and of learning."

"I quite agree," Margen said, somewhat surprised at the spymaster's philosophy. "In fact, it was one reason I came to work for the king."

"To teach magic," Hewlitt said. "That's a lofty goal, but it requires students."

"Miss Kendral seems to have not only recognized but capitalized on that," Margen said. "My class is just one of six at her academy." Margen cocked an eyebrow toward the spymaster. "And you've already talked with her about expansion and funding."

"Yes," Hewlitt agreed. "But my experience is that, even with this institute, there will always be more jobs for mages than there are mages."

"Yes," Margen agreed. "To become a mage takes time, dedication, and skill."

"As I'm learning," Hewlitt said.

"And so what has this to do with your proposition?"

King's Crown

"This train we're riding on results from the application of magic to a particular problem," Hewlitt said, waving a hand at the plush cushioned seats on which they were riding. "Mostly it was built by men who have no magic."

"Yes," Margen said encouragingly. "And?"

"The tracks could be laid without magic," Hewlitt said. He raised a hand to forestall Margen's reply, adding, "It would be slower but possible."

"Yes," Margen agreed reluctantly.

"The same cannot quite be said for the airships," Hewlitt continued, "because they need mages to provide the lift. But once aloft, the mechanical steam engines are their sole source of power."

"Are you suggesting that we could discover a non-magical way of raising airships?"

Hewlitt's eyes widened, and he shook his head. "I wasn't suggesting that although it is *quite* an interesting proposition, isn't it?"

"I suppose," Margen said, full of reluctance. "But then we'd need fewer mages, not more."

Chapter Five  113

"We'd need fewer *airship* mages," Hewlitt countered, "which means we'd have more mages to employ elsewhere."

"And where might they be employed, then?"

"It's possible to store spells on certain metals and jewels, is it not?" Hewlitt asked.

"Of course," Margen agreed. "But a stored spell is never as good as a fresh one."

"But for people who don't have magic, it's much better than nothing," Hewlitt said. "And if we could come up with a number of sensible spells that people would want and create them in sufficient number, we would be performing a most useful service to the people of our land."

"Selling magic, is it?"

"Selling magic rings and amulets," Hewlitt said. "Consider this: a ring that could cast a light."

"People have torches and candles for that," Margen said.

"But there are many times when they don't," Hewlitt replied. "And times when it's windy or rainy, extinguishing those handy lanterns and candles."

"And if we could make enough of them, and cheap enough, the rings might prove more valuable than torches or

candles," Margen muttered to himself. He raised his eyes to Hewlitt and gave the spymaster a firm nod. "Very well, what else?"

Peter Hewlitt suppressed a smile as he plunged into his list of possible ring spells, watching the mage grow more and more excited with each new revelation. Finally, he sat back in his chair and said, "So, do we have an agreement?"

"Oh, very much so!" Margen chortled, extending a hand to the spymaster who took it firmly. "I believe this marks the beginning of a glorious adventure!"

Chapter Five

116 King's Crown

Chapter Six

"e heard nothing," the Kingsland officer told them, with misery in his eyes. He told them that he was Ensign Rivers. "We fired and fired and heard no sound."

"Why?" General Dartan asked, his voice hard. He had had one of his men take Babette Colette away to another tent so that she wouldn't be troubled by the interrogation. They'd had to wait until the afternoon to get the ensign sober enough to talk.

"The King said that your soldiers killed Queen Airivik, that you had forfeited all rights and that, because no one would take the blame, he would take a thousand lives for hers."

"And you didn't think to question this?" an officer shouted in outrage.

"Would you, sir, have questioned your King in front of your commanding officer?" the ensign asked. "And the king's

mage was there, as were his apprentices." He shook his head. "It wasn't my place to question it."

"But you felt guilty," General Dartan said.

The hangdog man met his eyes for just an instant and dropped his head in shame, nodding slowly. "In war, that's one thing…"

"And you must have wondered, if he could do this to prisoners, what would he do to you if you disobeyed his order?"

"No," Ensign Rivers said, "I knew he'd kill me." He pursed his lips as if to say more, paused, then said in a rush, "I'd heard about the cavalry."

"Cavalry?"

"Colonel Walpish and his troopers," Traver said.

"What of them?"

"The king rewarded them for capturing the assassin," Rivers said.

"So they *caught* him!" one of the officers exclaimed.

"He wore the uniform of a Sorian colonel," Rivers said. "At least that's what I heard."

"You sound doubtful," Dartan said.

"Because the king gave the colonel and his best men new leather jackets, red leather," Rivers said.

"So?"

"And when the cavalry left to go north, every man wearing the new jackets was killed by an assassin," Rivers said.

"They were set up!"

"That's what I think now," Rivers agreed. "Before, my captain told me that it was probably a Sorian — " he gave the men surrounding him an apologetic look " — some holdout assassin."

"And now what do you think?" Murat, the soldier who'd been sent to guard little Babette Collet, asked.

"I think my captain was wrong," Rivers admitted miserably.

"If your king were to offer you a new jacket?" Dartan asked.

"I'd be happy to give it away," Rivers said.

"Listen," Dartan said, leaning in closer to the ensign, forcing him to meet his eyes, "your king betrayed his honor,

Chapter Six 119

he ordered you to kill innocent men. What are you going to do about it?"

"I don't know, what can I do?" Rivers asked, meeting the enemy general's eyes frankly.

"What would you do if it was our king, and he did that to your comrades?" Murat demanded heatedly.

"I'd kill him," Rivers said. "I would break my parole and get my men to revolt."

General Dartan waited a long moment before he asked, in a quiet voice, "Ensign, are you willing to regain your honor?"

"Ahoy the deck!" The lookout called from atop the central balloon of the airship *Wasp*. "Smoke cloud, dead ahead!"

"Get me my glass!" Captain Fawcett cried, moving to the bow of the airship. A sailor rushed the spyglass up to him and Fawcett snapped it out of his hands, bringing it to his eye and scanning the horizon. He was interrupted a moment

  King's Crown

later by someone jostling his shoulder and turned irritably to berate the idiot who'd disturbed him.

It was Lewis. "What do you see?"

"Smoke," Fawcett said, raising the glass to his eye once more. "A high plume."

A dull booming sound came to their ears.

"There's been an explosion," Lewis said. He gestured for Fawcett to pass him the looking glass. The airship captain passed it over without a word and waited, impatiently, while the cavalry officer completed his scan.

"Maybe an earthquake?" Lewis muttered to himself. He lowered the glass, passing it back to Fawcett and said, "Captain, the king will buy you a new ship. We *must* get to Korin's Pass now!"

"Stokers!" Fawcett shouted to the men working at the stern. "Full speed ahead!"

"We'll run out of fuel, sir!" the first mate called back.

"We'll feed the flames with whatever wood we can spare, have a crew armed with axes," Captain Fawcett shouted in reply. He turned back forward, raising his glass and muttering

Chapter Six 121

to Lewis, "We'll get there as soon as we can. I just hope you're right about the king."

"Well, the dust seems to be settling," Margaret said to Ellen Annabelle as she peered down from atop her wyvern friend. "I'd say that Freddie might not know his powers, really."

Beneath her, the twin-souled wyvern rumbled in agreement. The wyvern craned her neck around so that she could see Margaret, then dipped a wing down and started a marvelous curling descent.

"Wait!" Margaret cried, pulling on the wyvern's neck. "Over there!"

Wyvern and rider turned and then soared upwards high in the sky for a better view.

"What's that?" Margaret said, pointing to a dot in the distance, growing larger.

King's Crown

"How's the train line?" Moira Kendral asked spymaster Hewlitt when they met at the train station as the spymaster, mage Margen, and the railcrew returned.

"With Margaret's help, we managed to lay a full league," Peter Hewlitt told her. He raised an eyebrow. "Why do you ask?"

"We should talk about it later," Moira said. "Alone."

"In the meantime, the spymaster has come up with a brilliant idea," Margen said, rubbing his hands in glee. "An undertaking of the most profitable sort."

"Really?" Moira said, sounding doubtful.

Margen turned to Hewlitt. "Can I tell her?"

"Perhaps it's best if we wait to be certain of our production lines," Hewlitt said. He turned his attention to Mrs. Kendral. "May I ask, dear lady, why it is you greet us here at the train station and not, say, at the Reedis Memorial Academy?"

"I took a look at Brookes' accounts," Moira said, her expression harsh.

"Ah," Hewlitt said. He turned to Margen. "Mage Margen, perhaps it's best if you give me and this wonderful lady some time to confer alone." When Margen made to protest, Hewlitt cut him off with a raised hand, saying, "I suspect it will all be rather tedious for one such as you."

"And I'm *sure* your students will be eager for your return," Moira Kendral added enticingly. "There are cabs just outside, if you need."

"Of course," Margen said. He beamed at Hewlitt. "And perhaps I shall start the students on the new project when I get back."

"An excellent idea!" Hewlitt agreed. He waved Margen toward the exit and offered an arm for Mrs. Kendral, adding, "Where should we talk?"

"Mr. Brookes has an office," Moira Kendral said, ignoring Hewlitt's arm and, instead, leading the way. "I'm afraid it's desperately in need of a cleaning and it's rather dark."

"Some candles, perhaps?" Hewlitt suggested as Mrs. Kendral paused in front of a drab door.

Mrs. Kendral smiled and opened the door, while rummaging with her other hand in her purse. "I've got something better."

She pulled a small fire demon out and lofted it high into the room. Its brilliant light seemed overwhelmed by the size of the room.

"This is the front office, the books are back there," Mrs. Kendral said, pointing toward another door at the far end of the room.

"By all means, lead on," Hewlitt told her with a smile and a wave of his hand.

"On deck!" a voice called down from the crow's nest. "Strange sighting dead ahead!"

"Well, man, what is it?" Captain Fawcett called back irritably.

"It looks like—" the man faltered "—it looks like a small dragon, sir. Maybe a cloud."

"A cloud?"

"But it's moving toward us, sir," the nervous lookout called back.

"Let me see!" Fawcett grumbled, racing forward once more to the bow. A midshipman was sent trotting after him with the spyglass. Fawcett took it from him and trained it forward. "I don't see — wait!" He lowered the glass and shouted the length of the deck. "Beat to quarters! Man all guns!"

"What is it?" Major Lewis asked, trotting toward Fawcett.

"I don't know, but I'd prefer to be prepared," Fawcett told him. He waved at the bow. "First, we see an immense cloud of smoke and now we see this."

"You're thinking maybe the dragon set fire to a village?" Lewis asked, his eyes going wide.

"Captain Ford in *Spite* hit one, I've no doubt we can, too," Fawcett said, his eyes going hard as he watched his men race to their stations. Captain Fawcett moved closer to the cavalry officer as he added in confidence, "I'd truly love to have *something* to fight right about now!"

Lewis gave him a worried look.

"What?" Captain Fawcett demanded.

"Well, wouldn't it be better to find out what's up before starting a battle?" The cavalry officer asked in reasonable tones.

"Do you suppose that dragon asked the village?" Fawcett snapped back, turning away from the cavalry officer and moving down the deck to encourage his sailors as they manned their guns.

"Fixer!" Ibb shouted as soon as he entered the cavernous halls of the metal immortal. "Fixer, show yourself!"

Silence.

"I shall make lights," Tracker said, raising her hands and moving them in intricate patterns. A moment later, two bulbs of light appeared where her hands had traced. She spoke to them and they ballooned into huge balls of brilliant light even as she sent them high up into the space above them.

Rabel and Angus both gasped at the sight that came to their eyes. The cavern was a ruin. Metal shards littered the floor, the high gantries and other edifices were all crashed

upon each other, resting drunkenly atop other ruins. Hana glided up on a shaft of air and landed quietly behind them, her dark eyes taking in everything.

"We must find Fixer," Ibb said, plodding through the detritus in front of them.

"Wait!" Tracker called. The others stopped and turned toward the cylindrical immortal. "That is my job."

"Well, do not let us delay you," Ibb said tightly.

Tracker moved forward, scanned the area and pointed one thin arm decisively at a mound of broken metal. "That is Fixer." A moment later, she pointed in another direction. "And that." With an anguished cry, a second later she added, "And that, and that, and that, and that, and —"

"Shush now, Tracker, we get the picture," Angus said, moving up beside the distraught immortal and resting a hand lightly on her metal shoulder.

"Rabel, if you would help me collect her," Ibb said, moving forward to the last pile of scraps Tracker had indicated.

"We should be aware of traps," Rabel warned, waving his hands in a complex pattern in the air.

 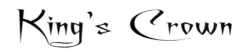 King's Crown

"Why would anyone do this?" Angus asked as he knelt down and started sorting through the largest pile of Fixer's remains.

"To cripple us," Ibb said. He picked up a small pile of gears and gently stepped back to deposit them with Angus' pile.

"Cripple or destroy?" Rabel asked, moving forward toward another pile of remains. "Who can rebuild Fixer?"

"Fixer," the two metal immortals said in unison.

"And, failing that," Rabel asked softly, "who else?"

The two metal men were silent. After a long moment Ibb spoke, turning to Tracker. "I believe we shall have to make a deal."

"Yes," Tracker said. "That is the obvious, predictable outcome."

Ibb's eyes flared brighter. "Are you saying this was planned to force our reaction?"

"I am not sure," Tracker said. "If this was meant to destroy us, a more thorough destruction would have been indicated. If meant only to cripple and force us into a bargain,

Chapter Six 129

then merely incapacitating Fixer beyond our own means of restoration would be sufficient."

"This seems more than that," Ibb said, gesturing at the destruction around them.

"Then, logically, the assailant wanted to do more," Tracker said.

"Not just cripple, but delay," Rabel guessed.

"Which," Tracker said in agreement, "means that delay is important."

"This is my hunt," Hana said. "Lyric — or whoever controls her — caused this to happen."

"And wants to delay you," Ibb said in agreement.

"I will go with you," Tracker declared.

"And I," Angus said, moving to stand beside the young woman, his hand within easy reach. Hana smiled and took it, clasping it tightly, even as she nodded toward Tracker, "I am grateful for your offer."

"Ibb and I will collect Fixer and get her to rights," Rabel declared.

"Sadly, I cannot," Ibb said.

"What?"

"I must warn the others," Ibb said. "What I have seen here may not be forgotten."

"Indeed," Tracker agreed. She looked at Rabel. "You are the best experienced among the humans in this sort of reconstruction."

"But it might take years!" Rabel protested.

"Thus making certain that it will be a job well done," Ibb agreed.

Rabel shot an exasperated look toward Angus, but the other was intent on Hana. With a groan, Rabel threw up his hands. "Fine! I'll get help from Ophidian."

"I cannot put Fixer in debt, I have not that right," Ibb said.

"You forget that we are already in debt, and that this was intended," Tracker reminded the other immortal softly. A moment later she added, "And who do you suppose arranged this debt, wise Memory?"

Ibb's chest rumbled in reflection of his irritation.

"You must get Jarin Reedis on this," Ibb said. "And the zwerg engineer, the one helping with the airship —"

"What airship?" Angus asked in surprise.

Chapter Six 131

"She has the abilities, she worked with Fixer some decades back," Ibb continued, ignoring the young human.

"Yes, as did I," Rabel said, his humor returning. "Very well, before we separate, I ask that you all help me gather Fixer."

"Of course," Ibb said, moving forward toward the next pile of Fixer's ruined body.

"Ah, First Minister Mannevy," Prince Sarsal exclaimed when he caught sight of the man, "I was hoping to find you!"

"You were?" Mannevy asked in surprise. The Crown Prince was carrying a tray with two beautifully crafted glasses set upon it. In his other hand he had an old, dusty bottle — apparently some rare vintage of wine.

"I thought you should be the one," Sarsal said mysteriously.

"The one for what?"

"Why to give my mother and our new king the royal toast!" Sarsal said, cheerfully. He dipped his head to add conspiratorially, "You know, they've ducked out of sight

King's Crown

and I imagine—" he broke off, reddening. "Well, let's just say that they will probably be less than excited if I were to interrupt them."

"And you want me to have that honor?"

"Well, it *is* the royal toast," Sarsal said in a huff. "Thousands of years of tradition that the king and queen drink from the royal goblets—" he dipped the tray suggestively "—and drink the special wine from the royal vaults."

"Oh, I see," Mannevy said, reaching for the tray, "very well, then."

"I've already opened the bottle, as you can see," Sarsal said helpfully. "Get them each to drink and wish them the health of their realm."

"Very well, my prince, I believe I can do that," Mannevy said, reaching for the bottle which the prince promptly passed to him.

"I'm sure you can," Crown Prince Sarsal said with a broad wink, turning away and rushing back to the festivities.

Chapter Six 133

"Everything in order?" Melodie asked sweetly as she stepped out of the shadows and joined Sarsal as he entered the royal hall.

"Couldn't be better," Crown Prince Sarsal said, smiling at her. "And you?"

"All done," she replied primly. "Should be quite a show in about an hour."

"Really?"

"First, they all get roaring drunk, some will vomit —"

"Vomit?"

"— not enough to do any good," Melodie hastily assured him, "and then not long after that… they'll die."

"And thus ends the Kingsland Army," Crown Prince Sarsal said with a gleam in his eyes. He glanced toward Melodie. "And us?"

"Take this now and you'll be fine," she said, handing him two small pills.

"And you?"

"Already taken, my dear."

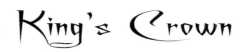

"Gunners, stand ready!" Captain Fawcett shouted as the flying beast zoomed toward them.

"Really, Captain—" Major Lewis began.

"I've already told you, sir, I'll not hazard my command on a hope!" Fawcett barked. "Now, if you continue to insist on making a nuisance of yourself, you may go below."

Major Lewis took a step back, furious. His hand went to the sword at his side. "May I remind you, sir, that this mission was assigned to me!"

"This has nothing to do with your mission!"

"Precisely!" Lewis replied, lowering his hand and moving closer to the airship captain. "We do not have the steam, nor the time, to engage in this frivolous —"

"On deck!" the lookout called from above. "There's someone *riding* the beast!"

Fawcett and Lewis both looked up and called back. "What?"

Fawcett gave Major Lewis a fulminating look and continued, "What sort of person?"

Chapter Six

"It looks like—" the lookout returned slowly "—well, sir, it looks like a girl."

Fawcett glanced at Lewis. "Have you ever heard of someone riding a dragon?"

Lewis shook his head. "I'd never heard of dragons until that complete mess at Korin's Pass."

"And this dragon comes from Korin's Pass," Fawcett said.

"Lookout, is the beast a dragon or a wyvern?" Lewis called up, cupping his hands over his mouth for a loud-hailer. He added quickly, "Does it have two legs or four?"

"Two, sir," the lookout called down.

"So," Lewis said to Fawcett, "*not* a dragon."

"The beast is white with a tint of purple," the lookout added.

"The dragon was black with red," Lewis said to Fawcett. He gestured to the men tensely standing by their cannon. "Perhaps we should stand them down, to avoid any accidents."

Fawcett chewed his lip angrily and then, with an abrupt nod, called out, "Stand down but stand ready!"

"Sir, the beast is rising!" the lookout called. "I can't see it, the sun's blinding!"

Fawcett shot Lewis an angry look. "It could dive on us and we'd be defenseless."

"True," Lewis allowed with a shrug. "But having your men at the guns won't help in that case." He gestured for the air mage who came striding over to them. "If the wyvern attacks, can you defend us?"

Before the young mage could answer, there was a thump above them and the balloon sagged for a moment just as the lookout cried in alarm.

"Back to your guns!" Fawcett shouted to his men.

"Deck there!" the lookout called down. "Sir, you won't believe this. I've two girls here who want to talk with you."

"*Two* girls?" Fawcett repeated in surprise. He glanced at Lewis. "How will they get down? They can't climb the rigging!"

"They're coming down the rigging!" the lookout called from above. "They're requesting parley." A moment later, the lookout added in confusion, "The littlest one is the wyvern, sir."

Chapter Six 137

Fawcett shot Lewis an accusing look, but the Major shrugged, unable to offer any advice.

The little girl scampered down the ratlines as though she'd been born on the sea — or in the air. The taller, older girl moved more carefully, but when she stumbled and seemed doomed to fall to her death, she merely squeaked and bounced back to the lines, holding on more tightly.

"Really, Margaret, why don't you just *float* down?" the little girl's piping voice carried down to the deck where the crew were milling nearby, looking both worried and amazed.

"Are you an air mage?" Lewis called up.

"I know you, you're the one Vistos called 'useless'!" Fawcett's young air mage, Marsters, exclaimed. The other air mage climbed out of the hatchway and Marsters called to him, "Here, Warren, isn't that the one Vistos called useless?"

Mage Warren gave Margaret a cursory inspection and nodded.

"Vistos is dead," the little girl called back, jumping on the deck. She turned and scanned the crew. A moment later she smiled and moved straight toward Major Lewis. "You're Major Lewis, aren't you?"

Lewis didn't reply, an expression of terror on his face. "Sir, sir! What are you doing here?"

"Lewis," Fawcett said in a worried tone, "what is it?"

"Don't you see?" Lewis said, turning back to Fawcett and waving toward the little girl. "Don't you see him?"

"What I'd like to know, Major Lewis, is how *you* can see him," the little girl said. "I was told I'd have to make introductions."

"I'd know Colonel Walpish anywhere, miss," Lewis told her firmly. "But, sir, they said you were dead!"

"I'm afraid he is," the little girl said. "Tell me," she asked out of curiosity, "can you see her, too?"

"See who, miss?" Lewis asked. He seemed to recover, "And, may I ask, who are you?"

"Thomas Walpish is my protector," the girl said. "Ophidian tasked him with guarding me, along with Skara Ningan." She gestured to a spot of thin air just to the right of her, and Lewis gasped. The girl smiled grimly. "Mage Vistos killed them."

"Lewis?" Captain Fawcett began in a small voice. "Are you saying that you're seeing ghosts?"

Chapter Six ⚇139

"I'm Margaret Waters," the taller girl said, moving forward in front of the child. "I'm the wyvern rider." She smiled down at the girl. "And this is Ellen Annabelle, the wyvern."

"What about the ghosts?" Fawcett said, taking the older girl to be the most sensible at the moment. "Can you see them, too?"

"Of course," Margaret said with a smile. She nodded to her left. "Colonel Walpish, may I make you known to—" she broke off and her brows creased as she said, "Sir, whom am I addressing?"

"That's Captain Walter Fawcett," Major Lewis said with a wave of his hand. "And this is His Majesty's Airship, *Wasp*."

"Captain Fawcett," Margaret said with a nod and a quirk of her lips, clearly she was enjoying herself, "This is Thomas Walpish, late of the Kingsland Cavalry —"

Fawcett gasped as the air in front of him seemed to ripple and a figure appeared out of it.

Margaret continued, her dimple growing, as she waved to her right, "And this is Skara Ningan, formerly assassin in the King's employ."

 King's Crown

Fawcett gaped at the woman who'd appeared out of nothing.

"They are dead, sir," Ellen Annabelle said. "They died destroying mage Vistos." She stretched out her hands to Skara and Thomas, who smiled and took them in return. "Ophidian has asked them to guard me."

"Against what?" Mage Warren asked in amazement.

"The three-headed god wants her dead," Margaret Waters said, moving to stand before Ellen Annabelle. She gave the two other mages a grim smile. "That will not happen while I live."

King's Crown

Chapter Seven

**Y**ou understand what you're to do?" General Dartan said to the Ensign Rivers.

The young Kingsland officer nodded grimly. He looked down at Babette Colette. "I can't say that I like involving the child in this —"

"It's not your choice, sir," Babette told him defiantly. "It was not your father who was murdered."

Rivers started to reply, but the fierce look in the girl's eyes made him think better of it and he settled for a mere nod of his head.

"You with the girl could gain entrance where you with any other could not," General Dartan reminded him softly.

"And as soon as we're in, the soldiers will come for the weapons," Babette said with wicked satisfaction.

General Dartan gave her a sharp look. "Be careful, child, that you do not become that which you despise."

"I will do anything to see these Kingsland scum get what they deserve!"

General Dartan chewed his lip, wondering whether to reply.

"General, we haven't much time," Colonel Molet reminded him. "We need to move before the sun sets."

General Dartan sighed and nodded in agreement. "Very well, go and may the gods bless you!"

"And how much will you sell these rings for?" Moira Kendral asked as mage Margen proudly jiggled a handful of new-spelled copper rings in his cupped hands.

"How much?" Margen made a face and turned to Hewlitt.

"Mrs. Kendral, I was hoping I could enlist your aid in that project," Hewlitt responded with a suave bow of his head. "You have much talent in that arena."

"Hmph!" Moira snorted, not taken in by the flattery. She narrowed her eyes at the rings thoughtfully, then said, "Ten percent."

  King's Crown

"Five," Hewlitt replied immediately.

"Eight."

"Seven and a half."

"Deal," Moira said, extending her hand. Hewlitt shook it gladly. The innkeeper's wife and Nelly's mother smiled as she confessed, "I was willing to go as low as six."

"And I was willing to go as high as nine," Hewlitt told her with a grin.

Moira shook her head and turned her attention back to mage Margen. "So how many of these can you make a day?"

"Actually, I'm more interested in *what* we can make each day," Hewlitt said.

"You say seven and a half," Margen said, ignoring the two. They blinked. "Then the students must get twenty."

"Ten!" Moira and Hewlitt roared in unison.

The mage blinked in surprise. "I suppose ten per cent isn't too bad —"

"Mage Margen, I'm afraid you have not the right to negotiate on behalf of students of my college," Nelly Kendral said as she entered the kitchen. She shot a glance toward her

Chapter Seven 145

mother and waved a hand towards Margen's handful of rings. "Am I right in guessing this has to do with those?"

"Oh, now you've done it!" Moira told the two men with a cackle. Margen looked confused, but Hewlitt looked thoughtful. "I'm not a *patch* on her!"

"Uh, yes, we *were* talking about the spell rings," Margen said.

"Made in *my* school, with *my* materials, and on *my* time," Nelly said, moving closer and closer to Margen with each word. At the end, she scooped the rings out of his cupped hands and spilled them into a wide pocket at her side. "So those rings are *mine*."

"But they wouldn't have made them if I hadn't taught them," Margen complained.

Nelly turned on Hewlitt. "And why did he have the students make them?"

"Well," Hewlitt replied slowly, "because we wanted to make a lot in a hurry."

"A *lot?*" Nelly shouted, glancing toward her mother for support. "Do you know *nothing* about supply and demand?"

"Pardon?" Margen said, with an owlish blink.

"And you?" Nelly demanded of Hewlitt.

"This is just the first batch," the spymaster replied with just a touch of panic in his voice.

"And the *last* batch!' Nelly said.

"But, my dear—" Margen began.

"And how many students will I lose tomorrow?" Nelly demanded of him. "Now that they know how to do it, what's to keep them from doing it themselves?"

"Um… nothing," Margen admitted.

Nelly turned flashing eyes on Hewlitt. "Supply and demand!"

"Actually, I think it's a good thing," a new voice spoke up. Nelly spun toward the owner and took a step back in shock. "Jarin? Reedis?"

"Both of us," Reedis admitted as the twin-souled mage entered the room.

"Where have you been?" Nelly demanded.

"Listening," Reedis said, pointing to the corridor.

"And you think it's a good thing?"

"Yes," Reedis said. "Consider, how many people have you taught balloon magic?"

Chapter Seven 147

"That's… that's *beside* the point!" Nelly protested.

"No, my love," Reedis said, moving to engulf her in a hug, "that's exactly the point."

"Explain," Nelly said, allowing her tone to soften.

"We really want more people to know this," Reedis told her, "just as we want more people to know balloon magic. So that we can make more spell rings, so that we can lift more airships." He turned his head to Hewlitt. "And so we can build more rail lines and steam engines."

"To make Kingsland richer," Hewlitt said, nodding in understanding.

Reedis smiled at the spymaster. He looked down to his fiance. "And if you lose all your students tomorrow, just how many *new* students will be at your door in the morning?"

Nelly's eyes grew wide and then thoughtful.

"But what about the gods," Reedis continued thoughtfully. "I wonder how they will feel?"

"Well, some of them will be delighted," Ophidian spoke up, appearing instantly just beside the kitchen stove.

King's Crown

"Which means that others will be appalled," Margen added in a thoughtful voice. He turned to Ophidian. "Has this ever happened before?"

Ophidian's eyes grew dark. "In the God's War."

Chapter Seven

150 King's Crown

Epilog

Crown Prince Sarsal slammed open the double doors to the royal chambers uninvited. He smiled as he saw the shocked looks on the faces of the King and his mother, the Queen.

"Oh, sorry! I hope I'm not interrupting anything," he said as he moved toward them.

King Markel, eyes bulging, hand to his throat, face flushed and red, waved his free hand excitedly. Beside him, Queen Rassa's eyes widened even as she gestured imploringly to her one and only son.

"Oh," Sarsal said, with a huge grin, "perhaps I *am*." He was close enough now to bat his mother's hand down. "I wonder whatever could it be?" He turned to King Markel. "Certainly not what you were hoping for, I see."

The King turned to Queen Rassa.

"What's that?" Sarsal asked, leaning forward with a hand cupped to his ear. "Speak up, I can't hear you!"

The Queen fell backwards onto the bed, her arms limp. Markel gave his stepson one horrified look and tried to raise a hand toward him, but failed.

"Oh, that's it!" Sarsal said. "You're dying!" He nodded toward the King. "I was told that this is a most painful poison, and it gives you a lingering death." He pursed his lips. "Won't be much longer, though."

He turned toward the door and raised his voice. "Guards! Guards!"

A figure raced into the room and stopped, eyes wide.

"Yes," Sarsal said, "first minister Mannevy. Perfect."

"What is it?" Mannevy cried in alarm, moving toward the stricken royals.

Sarsal raised an arm to restrain him. "Don't tell me you don't know!" He waved at the King who had finally succumbed and joined his wife in death. "After all, you were the one who served them the wine!"

Mannevy's eyes went wide, and he licked his lips. "The wine? But you —"

King's Crown

"Poisoned them?" Sarsal asked. He nodded happily. "But, you see, dear first minister, no one will ever know. Because we all know that you brought them the drink."

"You're mad!"

"No," Sarsal said, pulling his dagger from its sheath and grabbing the first minister, "I'm King."

And he slashed Mannevy's throat with one quick motion. As the first minister crumpled to the floor, Sarsal buried the point of his blade in the dying man's heart. He took a moment to relish the tableau, then turned to the door and raised his voice.

"Guards! Guards! Come quickly! The King! The Queen!"

"It is night, you asked to be told," a guard called from outside the darkened caravan.

"How fares the weather?" Gamden Ikar called back, turning his sore body over and pushing himself out from under his sleeping furs.

"There is a mist on the ground and the moon is full," the guard replied.

"And our height?" Gamden demanded with a growl. It was easier to get into the air from a height. He lashed out with his foot and struck the backside of the other eagleman, Jaden Ostan. "Get up!"

"Captain Elwes says you'll be able," the guard replied. Gamden allowed himself a bitter smile: the guard was more scared of his captain than of the eaglemen — that needed fixing.

"My compliments to the captain and tell him that he's an ignorant dog not fit to lick my boots," Gamden replied.

The guard had no answer to that.

Ten minutes later, Gamden and Jaden were on top of the caravan, looking down into a valley — the captain had selected a good campsite and launching point.

The moon was full, and the ground covered in a low fog.

"A perfect night for flying," Gamden declared. He cocked his head at Jaden. "Isn't it?"

King's Crown

"Do we have enough height?" Jaden asked, glancing to the valley below.

"If you can't fly from this height, you deserve to die," Gamden told him contemptuously. "Come on, we have to look around." He saw Captain Elwes below and the rest of the guards lounging. To Jaden he added, "We'll show these ground-hoggers what it's like to soar."

He stepped back to the rear of the caravan, turned, and raced toward the far edge and the valley below. He hurled himself off the edge, roared with delight —

— and soared up into the cold air above.

A moment later, another shape joined him, flapping hard and steadily to gain height.

With his eagle eyes, Gamden Ikar glanced out over the valley, straining for any hint of light or encampment. He cawed to Jaden Ostan, indicating that they should spread out to cover more ground.

Ostan shrieked back and twisted down and away in a bank, widening the gap between them.

Epilog 155

Gamden soared upwards, his eyes straining over the ground below, when something caught his attention. He turned it. There! Light!

From a dim spark it became a brilliant flash, then a flare, a beacon of light. The light was purple-white, burning his eyes. He screeched in pain but arced toward it, determined to attack.

Shapes were rising from the ground!

He caught sight of wings, something flying. A challenge! He roared with delight and dove toward the ascending creature.

It was not a bird. It was not an eagle. With a flash of fear, Gamden Ikar spread his wings wide, straining desperately to avoid the intruder.

Another shape rose from the ground. And another. He recognized them. *Hexine!* The Duke was right!

With an angry cry, he dove again, determined to attack the hexine.

A warning shriek rose toward him, and a flash of purple-white grew brighter and larger.

King's Crown

Wait! A voice called. It seemed to shake the air and the very center of his being. Suddenly Gamden was blinded by a brilliant light. *This one will do no harm.*

"It is an eagleman!" A worried voice shouted in reply.

Yes, the voice agreed, *and much injured in its own way.* There was a pause, as if the voice were thinking. *Come with us, there is much to learn.*

Gamden screeched in protest.

"He's here to hurt the hexine!"

He does not have my permission, the voice replied.

A moment later, Gamden found a hand grabbing his wingtip, tugging at him. In amazement, he looked to see a young girl mounted on a flying shape — a wyvern. "Climb on," the girl called, tugging him closer. "You don't have the strength to fly all the way yourself."

Gamden cawed in protest, but it died in his throat. Fly where?

To my home, of course.

"That's the goddess Kahlas," the girl's voice explained. "I don't know why she wants you, but I think you don't really have a choice." The girl tugged again. "Let me pull you close

Epilog 157

and then you can change back. Bethany Margiss can carry us both."

Bethany Margiss?

"She's the wyvern," the girl explained. "I'm Chandra. People call me Earthshaker." She tugged again. "Really, you don't have a choice."

Goddess. Gamden could feel the truth in that. Kahlas was the goddess of the moon. Were they going to the Moon?

Yes.

END

  King's Crown

The Twin Soul Series

Currently spanning 20 books and over 200 characters, the Twin Soul Series keeps on growing!

If you'd like a list of characters, scan the QR Code below, it'll take you to the characters page on our website,

http://www.twinsoulseries.com

Acknowledgements

No book gets done without a lot of outside help.

We are so grateful to Jeff Winner for his marvelous cover art work.

We'd like to thank all our first readers for their support, encouragement, and valuable feedback.

Any mistakes or omissions are, of course, all our own.

About the Authors

Award-winning authors The Winner Twins, Brit and Brianna, have been writing for over ten years, with their first novel (*The Strand*) published when they were twelve years old.

New York Times bestselling author Todd McCaffrey has written over a dozen books, including eight in the Dragonriders of Pern® universe.

http://www.twinsoulseries.com

Printed in Great Britain
by Amazon

70391337R10092